"Alex," Sabrina said huskily, her eyes suddenly shadowed with doubt. "It's not just because of that passion you have for redheads, is it?

You don't have to pretend you care for me, but I'd like to know I mean more to you than that. Her lips were trembling as she tried to smile. "I have always hated to be just one of a crowd."

One hand reached out slowly to wrap itself in her long silky tresses. "Oh, no, love," he said. "I've never felt anything like this before in my life." His eyes were ebony stains in the bronze tautness of his face and his expression was oddly grave. "I've been thinking quite a bit lately about those redheads in my past. I remember reading a poem once about the 'mystic memory of things to come.' I've had a crazy notion since I met you that maybe there is such a thing. Perhaps I was subconsciously searching for my own sweet redhead among that faceless throng." A tender smile curved his lips. "You certainly took your time about appearing on the scene, sweetheart. I'd almost given you up."

Sabrina felt her throat tighten achingly and for a moment she couldn't speak. She'd expected a mocking reassurance, not this moving gift he'd given her with simple eloquence.

Alex tilted her head to look into her eyes. "I want to care for you, Sabrina. I want to wrap you in all the golden gauze of tenderness and velvet gentleness that still exists in this harsh world of ours. Will you let me cherish you, Sabrina?"

"Oh, yes," she said huskily, feeling a surge of love and delight that made her dizzy. "I want that, Alex."

WHAT ARE *LOVESWEPT* ROMANCES?

They are stories of true romance and touching emotion. We believe those two very important ingredients are constants in our highly sensual and very believable stories in the *LOVESWEPT* line. Our goal is to give you, the reader, stories of consistently high quality that may sometimes make you laugh, sometimes make you cry, but are always fresh and creative and contain many delightful surprises within their pages.

Most romance fans read an enormous number of books. Those they truly love, they keep. Others may be traded with friends and soon forgotten. We hope that each *LOVESWEPT* romance will be a treasure—a "keeper." We will always try to publish

LOVE STORIES YOU'LL NEVER FORGET
BY AUTHORS YOU'LL ALWAYS REMEMBER

The Editors

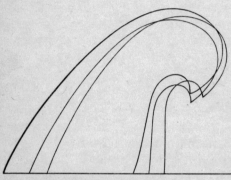

LOVESWEPT · 35

Iris Johansen

The Trustworthy

Redhead

BANTAM BOOKS · TORONTO · NEW YORK · LONDON · SYDNEY

THE TRUSTWORTHY REDHEAD

A Bantam Book / March 1984

LOVESWEPT and the wave device are trademarks of
Bantam Books, Inc.

ISBN 0-553-21627-9

Published simultaneously in the United States and Canada

Bantam Books are published by Bantam Books, Inc. Its
trademark, consisting of the words "Bantam Books" and
the portrayal of a rooster, is Registered in U.S. Patent and
Trademark Office and in other countries. Marca Registrada.
Bantam Books, Inc., 666 Fifth Avenue, New York, New
York 10103.

PRINTED IN THE UNITED STATES OF AMERICA

O   0 9 8 7 6 5 4 3 2 1

One

"Here you are, lady," the cab driver said cheerfully, as he slapped the arm of the meter down and peered curiously out of the windshield at the brilliantly lit entrance to the mansion. "Seems they're having a party." He gave a low whistle as his gaze traveled over the cars parked in the courtyard. "This looks like a combined Rolls Royce-Mercedes car dealership. *Very* nice!"

Sabrina smiled, amused by the man's admiration for those purely mechanical toys. He seemed not even to notice the magnificence of the mansion itself. "Yes, very nice," she agreed, as she drew her white velvet cloak about her, adjusting the hood carefully to shadow her face. "And you're quite right that there's a party here. It's a birthday party."

He got out of the cab and opened her door. "A birthday party," he repeated thoughtfully, as he helped her out and then reached across the back seat to pull out a large, tarpaulin-covered canvas. "This is a pretty hefty present for a little thing like you to be carrying. Would you like me to take it inside for you?"

Sabrina shook her head. "I'm stronger than I look." She handed him the fare and accepted the painting in return. "If you'll just ring the doorbell for me?"

"Sure thing," he said. Suddenly his eyes widened in surprise. "Birthday party," he said, snapping his fingers as he made the connection. "Didn't I read about some fancy party in the newspaper this morning? It was for that billionaire oil sheik who's set Houston on its ear in the last few years."

Sabrina nodded calmly. "Alex Ben Raschid. It's his grandfather who's the sheik. He's only the heir apparent to the Sheikdom of Sedikhan."

"He may not run the country yet, but he sure must run everything else," the driver said wryly, as he punched the bell in the recessed entry to the doorway. "Sedikhan Petroleum seems to be buying up every industry in sight."

He cast a knowing glance at the young woman standing quietly at his side. Now he could understand his passenger's presence at what must be an elite party. The apartment complex where he'd picked her up, while respectable, was inexpensive, and Ben Raschid had a very rakish reputation where beautiful women were concerned. Even with her face shadowed by the hood of her cape, he could tell this one was exceptionally lovely. The door was suddenly opened by a white-jacketed manservant and the driver touched his cap in a parting salute. "Good night, Miss. Have a nice evening." He turned and strode swiftly back to his cab.

"You have an invitation?" the butler asked politely.

"No." Sabrina shook her head as she reached in the pocket of her cape, withdrew an envelope, and handed it to the butler. "I was told to give this to Mr. Clancy Donahue."

The butler nodded. "If you'll wait in the foyer, I'll see if I can locate him for you immediately. I believe I saw him step into the library just a moment ago." He glanced at the canvas in her hands. "May I take that from you?"

"No, thank you," Sabrina answered, her hands tightening protectively on the canvas. "I was told to deliver it only to Mr. Donahue."

The butler frowned uncertainly. "Then perhaps you'd better come with me," he said. "I'm sure it will be all right. Will you step this way?"

The elegant foyer was almost deserted, but as she passed the open doors of the ballroom she caught a brief glimpse of motion and color and heard the mellow strains of a live orchestra. Then the butler was knocking discreetly on a carved teak door opposite the ballroom. He preceded her into a large book-lined room, lit only by a single brass desk lamp on a massive executive desk which was the central focus of the room.

"You wanted to see me, Josef?" a gravelly voice demanded from a bar in one corner, and Sabrina's gaze flew to the shadowy alcove as a man came forward into the pool of light before the desk.

"This young lady has a parcel to deliver, Mr. Donahue," the servant said, handing him the note and silently withdrawing.

She would never have pictured Clancy Donahue as an executive assistant. The man looked more like a prizefighter than a businessman. The dark tuxedo he wore only served to emphasize the burly toughness of his tall, massive figure. His blunt features were granite hard beneath curly brown hair, heavily streaked with gray. He appeared to be in his early fifties and the look he directed at her confirmed her supposition. The wisdom of hard-lived years shone in the ice blue eyes that assessed her with a hint of suspicion.

Then he swiftly read the letter before looking up with a frown. "You know what is in this letter, I presume, Miss"—he glanced down at the letter again—"Miss Courtney. I see that it's been in your possession for almost six months."

Sabrina shook her head. "No, of course not," she said, faintly shocked.

"Seeing that it was a personal letter from Princess Rubinoff concerning you, I'd say you've exercised admirable restraint," Donahue said dryly. "Particularly since Honey failed to seal it. Not many women could be trusted to stifle their curiosity to that extent."

"She knew I wouldn't read it," Sabrina said, a thread of indignation in her voice. "I met Honey at a gallery exhibition of her husband's work six months ago and we became very good friends. She knew very well I wouldn't violate that friendship."

"As I said, admirable," Donahue repeated. "It's very brief and to the point. It merely states that Honey has arranged a little birthday surprise for Alex and I'm to help in facilitating the giving of the gift in whatever way you may require." He lifted an inquiring eyebrow at the canvas in her hands. "I take it that's the gift in question?"

"No, this is Prince Rubinoff's gift," Sabrina said softly. "Honey entrusted it to me at the same time she arranged for her own present." She set the canvas down on the floor, leaning it carefully against the desk. "I've had it at my apartment for the last six months and I admit that I'm rather glad to be rid of it. It must be very valuable. Prince Rubinoff is so enormously famous now."

"Well, then what *is* the present that I'm to facilitate?" Donahue asked impatiently.

"Me," Sabrina said simply, as she slipped the hood from her head to reveal the dark, flaming shimmer of her long red hair. "I'm from Novelty-grams Incorporated, Mr. Donahue. I specialize in bellygrams. Honey paid me quite generously to perform a dance for Mr. Ben Raschid's birthday celebration. That's her gift to him."

"A belly dancer?" Donahue muttered, momentarily shocked out of his cynical coolness, "Good Lord, a belly dancer! And a red-haired belly dancer at that." Suddenly he started to chuckle. "Are you sure it wasn't Lance who put you up to this?"

Sabrina shook her head, a smile tugging at the corners of her lips. "I scarcely saw Prince Rubinoff after I performed at the gallery exhibition. He was closeted away completing a portrait for almost the entire week of their stay. No, this is Honey's idea entirely." She continued gently, "You needn't worry, Mr. Donahue, the sheik's guests won't find anything offensive in my performance. I've been very well trained." Her green eyes twinkled. "I solemnly promise you that there will be no bumps and grinds."

"If it's Honey's show, I'm not worried about that," Donahue replied, his expression still amused. "I presume you're in full regalia. Am I to be permitted an advance preview?"

"Of course," Sabrina said serenely, opening the cloak to reveal her midnight blue, chiffon costume.

The costume showed off her lush golden tan, and the flaming silk of her hair against the dark blue of the chiffon seemed almost to issue a tactile invitation. The outfit consisted of a comparatively modest bikini with sheer chiffon panels that floated gracefully to her ankles. The panels parted when she danced and her midriff was bare. The bodice of her costume, while not shockingly low, displayed a generous amount of cleavage.

Donahue gave an admiring whistle. "Lovely, absolutely lovely," he said sincerely. "You're an exceptionally beautiful woman, Miss Courtney." There was a hint of mischief in his broad grin. "I think I can guarantee that you'll be Alex's favorite present at this particular birthday party. I can hardly wait to see his face when he catches sight of you. When do we get this show on the road?"

"At the intermission when the orchestra takes a break," Sabrina answered, pulling a tape cassette out of the pocket of her cape and handing it to him. "Honey wanted the performance to come as a complete surprise. If you'll just take care of starting my music on Mr. Ben Raschid's stereo tape player, I'll introduce myself."

"Right," Donahue said, checking his watch. "That should be in about ten minutes. You'd better wait here in the library until I come for you. I'll tell Josef to stand guard and be sure no one comes in to disturb you." His lips curved cynically. "Though I doubt that even your charms would tempt that pack of sycophants away from Alex." He strode toward the door with surprising grace for such a large man. "Lord, I can't wait until he sees you!" The door shut quietly behind him.

Sabrina shook her head ruefully. Donahue's reaction of impish delight was the usual one, and most of the time her clients arranged for her particular messagegram as a practical joke. But the joke was almost always good-natured and she hadn't run into any real problems due to the slightly sexual overtones of her performance. She was paid far better than the other performers at Noveltygrams who did the various singing telegrams and balloongrams, and God knew she needed every penny she could scrape together these days.

She picked up the painting and carried it over to a massive, brass-studded, black leather armchair. Placing the canvas carefully on the seat of the chair, she unwrapped the tarpaulin, but scrupulously avoided the mocking dark eyes of the man in the portrait. It was strange the effect that face had exerted on her since the moment she'd seen it in Honey's hotel suite. It had filled her with a nameless uneasiness which hadn't faded with familiarity. There was something about those smoldering dark eyes that seemed to know all the secrets in the universe and was not about to reveal a single one of them. Combined with the lean forcefulness of that bone structure and the passionately sensual curve to those finely cut lips, the image was very disturbing.

It was to be expected that Prince Rubinoff would produce a portrait of his cousin that was dynamically alive, and this one was undoubtedly brilliant. Dressed in dark pants and a simple white shirt, open at the throat, he was half sitting, half leaning on a gray stone balustrade, his dark hair lifting in the breeze. His lips were curved in a cynical little smile. Alex Ben Raschid had the bold, dangerous look of a marauding corsair!

Dangerous? How fanciful could she get? Ben Raschid could represent no possible threat to her. In less than an hour she would have completed her performance and be on her way. Ben Raschid might be regarded as an economic shark in his own territorial waters, but she'd soon be swimming serenely away and be home with David before he could possibly gobble her up.

Not that he would want to, she thought wryly. According to the columns, Ben Raschid had more women panting at his heels than he could handle. He'd hardly be diverted by a pretty little dancer like herself for more than a passing moment. It was natural that her imagination had been stirred by having that mocking, enigmatic face constantly before her for the last six months, but he had no real connection with her own struggles and triumphs. Yes, she'd be glad to have this episode over, so she could rid herself of both the picture and the fascination it engendered.

"Miss Courtney." She looked up, startled, at Donahue standing in the doorway. "It's intermission. The orchestra will be breaking for the next twenty minutes."

"I'm coming," she answered, as she slipped off her white ballet slippers and once again pulled the hood of her cape over her hair. "I'll wait at the entrance of the ballroom until I hear my music. If you'll please turn on my tape?"

"Delighted," he said with a grin, his blue eyes twinkling. "Believe me, the pleasure is all mine." He disappeared and she quickly left the library and crossed the gleaming, oak parquet floor to stand in the open doorway of the ballroom.

Sabrina's lips pursed in a silent whistle of admiration at the sheer magnificence of the enormous room. It seemed to sing with color and light. The polished inlaid floor gleamed; a huge amber and crystal chandelier flowered like a brilliant blossom from the center of the ceiling. Exquisitely gowned women were fluttering within its sparkling light like colorful butterflies while men in somber tuxedos were their elegant foils.

Sabrina stood patiently, waiting for her music to begin. Suddenly she had the sensation of being watched, and with a strange feeling of inevitability she slowly turned her head toward a cluster of people at the far end of the ballroom.

Her gaze met that of Alex Ben Raschid, and for a moment she was only conscious of those ebony eyes holding her own across the room. Then his eyes traveled lingeringly over her body that was still enveloped in the white velvet cloak until they rested, with amused curiosity, on one shapely bare foot.

He was well over six feet with a whipcord

strength that was shown to advantage in a beautifully tailored tuxedo. His portrait really hadn't done
him justice, Sabrina thought dazedly. Ben Raschid
stood out in this artificial atmosphere like a candle in the darkness—totally virile, totally alive,
totally in command.

The familiar syncopation of her music throbbed
through the loudspeakers and she shook her head
as if to clear it. What was she doing gaping at the
man like a bedazzled teenager when she had work
to do? Even if she hadn't sincerely liked Honey
and wanted her gift to be really special, she always took pride in her performance.

She took a deep breath before gliding gracefully
to the center of the ballroom. The chatter of the
guests and the clink of crystal hushed abruptly.
She paused for dramatic effect, then pushed the
hood back from her hair. "Good evening," she
said softly. "I'm Sabrina Courtney. I've been sent
with a birthday greeting for Alex Ben Raschid
from Princess Rubinoff." Ignoring the sudden startled murmur from the guests, she slowly unbuttoned her cloak and let it fall from her shoulders
to form a pool of white velvet at her feet. She was
vaguely conscious that the murmuring became
startled gasps, but the volume of her music had
risen, and she began to dance.

She moved, turning, twisting, weaving graceful patterns that gradually built into a sinuous
and sensual excitement. She'd chosen the most
difficult dance in her repertoire, but it was also
the most enthralling. Somewhere along the way
she became one with the music, letting it carry
her into the most ancient and passionate of
rhythms. Nothing mattered but the dance and
the throbbing sound. Then, as the wild music
ended in a dramatic burst of chords, Sabrina fell
to her knees in the traditional position of obei-

sance before Ben Raschid. There was a moment of silence and then a tremendous burst of applause from the guests.

Sabrina smiled triumphantly. They had liked her! She threw back her head, her flaming, waist-length mane a tousled glory, and her emerald eyes radiant. "Happy birthday, Alex Ben Raschid," she said breathlessly. "Priness Rubinoff sends her regards and a message. She said to tell you that she's kept her promise." Then, as her eyes met his, she flinched involuntarily and lowered her eyes hastily.

Ben Raschid's eyes were alive with barely controlled rage and something else that filled her with bewilderment and alarm. She leaped gracefully to her feet, and amidst the still applauding guests ran lightly to the door of the ballroom and into the hall.

She had reached the front door before she realized she had completely forgotten her cape and slippers. What on earth was wrong with her, she wondered crossly? Ben Raschid hadn't spoken even one word to her and she was in a perfect panic over that stormy, yet enigmatic look. Perhaps the man had indigestion, for heaven's sake!

"You were a complete triumph," Donahue announced behind her. "You should have seen the expression on Alex's face while he was watching you dance. I've never seen anything like it!"

Neither had she, she thought uneasily, as with a feeling of relief she turned around to face him. "I'm glad you enjoyed it, Mr. Donahue," she said quickly. "I really do have to leave now. I wonder if I could trouble you to get my cloak from the ballroom while I go to the library and get my slippers?"

"That won't be necessary," Alex Ben Raschid said as he entered the hall, her white velvet cloak draped over his arm. He put it over her shoulders, carefully lifting her hair so that it flowed down her back in fiery contrast to the snow white velvet. His action had an odd intimacy to it, and Sabrina felt a little tingle of shock that was out of all proportion to what should have been her reaction to a courteous gesture. "You go on back to the ballroom and enjoy yourself, Clancy. I'll take care of Miss Courtney."

"I'm sure you will," Donahue said obliquely, as he turned back to the door of the ballroom.

"No, really, I don't need any help," Sabrina protested, feeling once more that tiny shudder of panic at the thought of being alone with Ben Raschid. "Please go back to your guests. I'll just go to the library and phone for a taxi."

"And get your shoes," Ben Raschid added, his gaze lingering on her bare feet peeping from beneath the cloak. "It's really a shame to cover them. I've always thought feet were the ugliest portion of the human anatomy, but yours are quite lovely." He glanced up at Donahue, who'd paused at the door at Sabrina's words. "I think I can be trusted to find Cinderella's lost slippers, Clancy. But you might make yourself available in about forty-five minutes to drive her home."

Donahue nodded with an expression of mild surprise on his face and disappeared into the ballroom.

Forty-five minutes? "No one needs to drive me home, Mr. Ben Raschid," she said hurriedly. "I can take a taxi as I intended. I really think you should return to the party."

The man was completely ignoring her, his hand beneath her elbow propelling her swiftly to the library. He shut the door behind them with a decisive click.

He leaned against it, his eyes on her face. "I assure you that the party will wait," he said softly.

"Though I'm not sure at the moment if I can." His hand reached out and touched the curve of her cheek. "Your face is really exceptional, do you know that? Those slightly tilted green eyes, that delicate, fragile bone structure are fascinating as hell."

She moved away from his hand, not wanting him to know how disturbing she found it, and laughed lightly to reinforce that effect. "So I've been told. My rather exotic look was one reason why Joel hired me."

"Joel?" Ben Raschid asked, his dark eyes flickering. "Who the hell is Joel?"

"Joel Craigen, my boss," Sabrina said. "He owns Noveltygrams Incorporated. Did you think this was a one-shot fling on my part? I do this all the time."

"I don't believe I was thinking at all," he said slowly, his face darkening. "Not from the time I saw you standing in the doorway looking like a barefoot nun. Do you mean you dance for other men like that?"

Sabrina frowned in puzzlement. "Of course I do," she answered. "The bellygrams are very popular. I have at least one assignment a day, sometimes two or three. It's what I do for a living."

He uttered a brief, obscene expletive that caused her eyes to widen with shock. "That will have to change," he said grimly. "Why the hell don't you go out and get a respectable job?"

"Respectable!" The word was a cry of indignation. "I don't think any of your guests found anything objectionable about my performance."

"None of the men at least," he snapped. "They were eating you up with their eyes. That dance was supposed to arouse every man in the room to fever pitch. You can't argue with that."

"I don't have to argue anything at all," she said,

fuming. "Not to you. I'm sorry you didn't approve of Honey's gift, Mr. Ben Raschid, I'm sure she'll be very disappointed. But as for myself, I couldn't care less what you think!" She turned and marched over to the leather armchair where she'd stepped out of her shoes. "I think I'll say good night now. I'm sure you're eager to get back to your more respectable guests."

"Dammit, I didn't say *you* weren't respectable," he said, following her across the room, his face stormy. "It's your occupation we were talking about, and I have every intention of making sure you care what I think from now on. Why do red-heads have to be so vol—" He broke off as his gaze fell to the portrait on the chair. "Where the hell did this come from?"

"I brought it with me," Sabrina said tersely, thrusting her feet into her ballet slippers. "It's your gift from Prince Rubinoff. I hope you like it better than you do his wife's."

"It's quite good," he said absently, as his gaze flicked back to Sabrina. "And Honey's present is also an enormous success. I couldn't be more pleased with her good taste. The wrapping is absolutely fantastic, and I can't wait to discover what's in the package."

"You've already received your gift," Sabrina snapped. "You seem to be under the misapprehension that the Princess contracted for more than just a dance for you." She moved toward the executive phone on the massive mahogany desk. "She bought my artistic services, not my body, for your delectation."

She reached out a hand to pick up the receiver but he stopped her by placing a swift hand over hers. "No," he said softly, a glimmer of steel beneath the satin of his voice. "I said that Clancy will take you home. I won't have you taking a taxi while you look like something out of an erotic dream. I'd take you myself if this party weren't more business than pleasure."

"You won't *let* me?"

"I won't let you," he repeated calmly. "Now, why don't you relax and humor me. It will save a good deal of wear and tear on your nerves. I'm not letting you out of here until I get you to answer a few questions. I'm curious why Honey sent you to me."

"But you know why she sent me," Sabrina answered, puzzled.

"Yes and no," he said absently, his eyes intent on her face. "I wonder if she really succeeded in her quest after all this time."

"Quest? I don't understand any of this."

"I know you don't, Sabrina," he said, smiling with a sudden warmth that was dazzling after the guarded somberness that had preceded it. "Don't worry about it. I'm going to make sure that everything will be quite clear to you very soon." He removed his hand. "Are you going to indulge my whim, pretty houri?"

"Do I have any choice?" Sabrina asked tartly. Her hand felt oddly lonely without the warmth of his covering it. Why was that, when his touch had so disturbed her? "Are you always this autocratic, Alex Ben Raschid?"

"So they tell me," he drawled mockingly. He leaned easily against the edge of the desk. "It will be practically painless, I promise you. Just give me all the details of your lurid past and I'll be more than happy."

"I doubt it," Sabrina said shortly. "My background isn't all that entertaining." Then, as he continued to wait patiently with that same enigmatic smile, she said resignedly, "I'm twenty-three years old. I was born and raised on a small ranch in the Rio Grande Valley not far from Corpus Christi. I'm an only child and both my parents died in an auto accident when I was sixteen. I attended the University of Houston for two years as an art major before I was forced to drop out and go to work. I'm self-supporting, hard-working, and independent." She cast him a glowering look. "And just as respectable as you, Mr. Ben Raschid."

"Alex," he prompted, with a grin. "And I'm sure you're a great deal more respectable. I've had a hell of a lot more years and opportunities to arrive at my present state of dissipation. This is my thirty-fifth birthday, you know."

She nodded impatiently, "Honey told me. Now that I've told you my entire life history, may I please leave?"

"I'm sure you've left out all the most interesting bits," Ben Raschid said dryly. "But I've always liked to make a few discoveries on my own. It makes a relationship that much more exciting."

"This is utterly absurd," Sabrina said, shaking her head in wonder. "How can I make you understand that I don't give a damn what you find exciting, or what you want?"

"I think that soon you'll care very much what I want," Ben Raschid said softly. "You see, I want you, Sabrina Courtney."

"This is crazy," she whispered, her green eyes widening with shock. "Thirty minutes ago you didn't even know I existed, and now you're propositioning me?"

"It's a bit of a shock to me, too." he said wryly. "I assure you my approach is generally a good deal more subtle." There was a flicker of anger in the depths of the coal black eyes. "You have an exceedingly odd effect on me, Sabrina, and I'm not at all sure I like it. This is the first time I've ever been caught off guard by my response to a woman."

"Should I apologize?" Sabrina asked caustically. Now that she'd recovered from her first shock at his words she was beginning to feel a rising anger at the sheer arrogance of the man.

Ben Raschid's brow rose. "Perhaps you should apologize at that," he drawled lazily. "I'm sure I'm not the first man your little performance has sent into a tailspin. You must be fully aware of your effect on the male libido." Suddenly the annoyance was gone, replaced by a dark intensity. His fingers reached out to trace the outline of her lips while she stared up at him in shocked amazement. "You have the most provocative mouth I've ever seen," he said huskily. "And your skin has the satin texture one sees only in very young children. I've never wanted to possess anything as much as I want you. You're going to belong to me in every way a woman can belong to a man."

Sabrina found it hard to breathe and she felt a tingling in the tips of her fingers. She shook her head to clear it of its strange lightness. "And what about what *I* want?" she asked, steadying her voice with an effort.

"I can make you want me," he said arrogantly. "Stay with me tonight, Sabrina. You won't regret it."

"Yes, I would," she said quietly. "I have no desire to be one of your conquests, Mr. Ben Raschid. I'm sure you can find someone else who will accommodate you. I don't want anything to do with you."

"And I want everything to do with you," he returned lightly. "But I can give you a little time." His hand reached out to stroke her cheek, seeming to take a sensual pleasure in its satin smoothness. "I'm not going to be able to wait very long," he whispered, his eyes flickering with that same hot intensity that had frightened her in the ballroom.

"You'll have to wait forever," she said tartly. "I don't intend to be one of your women. There's nothing about the position that appeals to me, even for the short time you usually keep your mistresses."

He smiled in genuine amusement. "I don't think you should count on anything but a very long-term lease. I don't believe I'll tire of you easily." His hand moved to her throat, not caressing, just resting lightly on the pulse point as if to detect the tumult of emotions cascading through her. "A very exclusive contract," he continued quietly. "No other men in your life or your bed while you belong to me."

What kind of woman did he think she was, she wondered wildly, caught in a bewildering maze of emotions. He was calmly giving her ultimatums and conditions, and completely ignoring her protests as if it were a foregone conclusion that she would give in to his demands.

His confidence was so complete that she wondered for an instant if her defenses could hold against this man's determined assault. But she knew they must. It would be like living in a silk cocoon whose strands would eventually strangle any independence or self-respect life might hold for her. She lifted her chin and looked up at him defiantly. "I'll have as many men as I like, but you won't be one of them, Alex Ben Raschid."

His hand tightened on her throat until it was not a caress but a threat, and his dark eyes blazed with anger. Then he slowly released her and stepped back. "I'd better send you home before I decide to keep you here," he said tightly. "I'd prefer to have you willing."

"Do you usually go in for slavery?"

One corner of his lips lifted in a flash of humor. "I couldn't have chosen anyone more suitably dressed for it," he said dryly. "No, my dear houri, I promised you time to get used to the idea but I'm beginning to regret my forbearance already. I think we'd better get you out of here." He opened the library door, and then, as she would have passed through it, he detained her momentarily by placing a hand on her arm. "It's only a reprieve, you know, Sabrina," he said softly.

She didn't answer as she sailed past him into the hall.

Donahue was standing by the ballroom door as if in anticipation, and at Ben Raschid's nod he smiled and came toward them, swallowing the last of his champagne and placing his glass on a passing waiter's tray.

"Take the young lady home, Clancy." Ben Raschid met his employee's eyes meaningfully. "And take good care of her."

Donahue nodded silently.

Ben Raschid turned to Sabrina. "I'll be in touch," he said softly, with an intimate smile.

Sabrina shrugged, feeling more courageous in the public atmosphere of the hallway. "Don't bother," she said coolly. "I plan to be very busy."

There was a choked sound from Donahue that might have been a chuckle, and she could almost feel the anger that emanated from Ben Raschid. "I'll be in touch," he repeated, this time menacingly. He turned and stalked back into the ballroom.

"My lady," Donahue said, with a mocking bow. "Your carriage awaits."

Two

Now that the evening was almost over, Sabrina felt numb with weariness. She leaned her head against the padded headrest of the luxurious Lincoln and closed her eyes. They had almost reached the apartment complex where she lived when Donahue spoke, as if unable to control his curiosity any longer. "Why did you try to make him angry?" he asked.

Sabrina's eyes flew open, and she made a face. "I didn't try," she said dryly. "It seems to come naturally."

Donahue shook his head. "People just don't talk to Alex Ben Raschid like that."

"Perhaps if they did, he wouldn't be so arrogant. Are you afraid of him, Mr. Donahue?" she asked tartly.

"Hell, no," he replied promptly. "We go back too far for that. I've known Alex since he was a teenager." There was an element of warning in his sideways glance. "But I can see why it might be wise for a pretty little thing like you to be a bit more cautious. Growing up as heir apparent to one of the richest oil sheikdoms in the world isn't likely to make any man shy and retiring. Even now he's one of the most powerful economic figures in the world. When his grandfather dies, he'll also be the absolute monarch of a country in his own right. It's only fair to warn you that Alex isn't hesitant about using that power."

Sabrina sighed tiredly. "Mr. Ben Raschid will have no problem with me; I won't get in his way. As a matter of fact, I'll stay just as far away from him as the Houston city limits permit!"

"Or Alex will permit," Donahue corrected wryly.

"In a day or two he'll forget I ever existed," Sabrina predicted confidently. "We don't belong to the same world."

"I wouldn't be too sure of that," Donahue said. "I've never known him to be so protective of a woman before. Usually he couldn't care less what his little playmates are up to as long as they're available when he wants them."

Donahue turned into the apartment complex and stopped in front of the building she indicated.

"Don't bother to get out," Sabrina said, with her hand on the door latch. "Thank you for bringing me home."

"Sit still, Miss Courtney." Donahue grinned. "I have my orders. Alex wants you delivered safely to your front door." He was around the car, gallantly helping her out with mocking panache and following her to the apartment door. He took her key when she withdrew it from the pocket of her cloak and unlocked the door. He said quietly, handing the key back, "Lock the door behind you."

"I will," Sabrina promised. "Thanks again, Mr. Donahue. You've been very kind."

"Sabrina, is that you?" Light suddenly flooded the apartment.

"Yes, David, I'll be there in just a minute," she called. Turning to Clancy Donahue she said hastily, "Good night."

"David," Donahue echoed thoughtfully, scanning the nameplate by the door. "David Bradford,

Sabrina Courtney." He gave a low whistle. "Alex may have more problems than he imagines."

"Please go," Sabrina whispered. David could be as curious as a chipmunk. He'd be out here any minute wanting to know who'd brought her home.

"Jealous, is he?" Donahue grinned. "Well, mum's the word. Good night, Sabrina." With a friendly wave of his hand he strode swiftly back to the car.

With a relieved sigh, she slipped inside and closed the door, locking it automatically behind her.

Angelina Santanella looked up from the horror movie she was watching with avid fascination. "You're later than usual, aren't you? David's been somewhat anxious."

"It's only a little after eleven," Sabrina answered, coming forward to perch on the arm of the heather tweed couch. "Where is he?"

"In the kitchen making himself a cup of hot chocolate," Angelina said, leaning forward to turn down the volume on the set. "I brought up a plate of coconut macaroons and they're practically all gone." She smiled broadly. "That boy surely does like his sweets."

"You spoil him, Angelina," Sabrina said, shaking her head reprovingly at the motherly-looking woman. The Santanellas occupied the apartment downstairs and their generosity was ample and open-hearted. "He's come to expect something from you every time you walk through the front door."

"*I* spoil him? That's the pot calling the kettle black. He washed his hair tonight and had me braid it for him in that heathen-looking pigtail he's so fond of." She frowned. "You know, you should make him cut his hair, Sabrina."

"He likes it," Sabrina said simply, "and it's no real bother."

The older woman shook her head, her face gentle.

"Nothing's a bother for you where that boy's concerned, is it? You've practically arranged your entire life around him."

"I love him," she said quietly. "He's closer than a real brother could ever be to me. And now he's my child as well."

"He does have parents of his own," Angelina reminded her, her dark eyes grave. "It's not right that you should have to shoulder the entire responsibility. It's too much, Sabrina."

"No it's not. You can't put limits on how much you give when you really care about someone. Jess and Sue do all they can. I'm the logical one to take care of David. He has to be near the drug rehabilitation center, and how could Jess and Sue possibly leave the ranch? It's not only their livelihood, it's where their roots are."

"They could help out financially a little more," Angelina persisted stubbornly. "You could get a safe, respectable job if you didn't have to worry about money all the time."

Respectable! It was the second time tonight she'd heard that word and she wasn't up to defending her job again at the moment. "His parents send what they can. The drought last year almost ruined them and they're just starting to recover. Besides it's *I* who owe them," Sabrina said simply. "They took me into their home without a second thought after my parents were killed. Jess and Sue owned the next property and David and I grew up like brother and sister. They certainly had no obligation to do all that for me!" She smiled cheerfully. "Besides, we get along very well. I make fairly good money at Noveltygrams and what David makes working for your husband pays his doctor bills."

"I know what Gino pays that boy and it's not enough to make a dent in that fancy psychiatrist's bill you get every month," Angelina said shrewdly. "You may be fooling the boy that he's helping out, but I keep the books." She sighed. "We'd like to pay David more but we just can't afford it. Maybe next year when the business is on its feet. David's worth three times what we're paying him. Gino says the boy has a green thumb."

Sabrina was well aware that Gino's Landscape Company was a fledgling enterprise. She was just grateful that Gino had found a place for David; it scarcely mattered that they could afford to pay him only a pittance. David genuinely loved working outside with his plants and flowers.

"How can we expect more from you and Gino?" she asked affectionately. "You've not only made a place for David in the company, but you're always cooking some delicacy for him. You even stay with him in the evening when I have to go out."

"He's no trouble," Angelina said gruffly. "He's such a good boy." There was a suspicious brightness in the liquid darkness of her eyes as she said hesitantly, "It's been so long. Is David ever going to be entirely well?"

"The doctors don't really know," Sabrina said huskily. "They don't have enough knowledge about the effect of so-called 'mind-expansion' drugs on the brain to really tell. He's come so far that I'm almost afraid to hope for more." She shivered. "When the ambulance took him to the hospital from the dorm that night, he was almost a vegetable." She stood up, and tried to smile brightly. "Well, you tell that 'good boy' when he finishes gobbling his cookies, that I'm in the shower, will you?" She shrugged off her cape and folded it over her arm. "Are you going to finish your movie before you leave?"

Angelina nodded as she leaned forward to turn up the volume on the set. "I think I will," she said, her expression already absorbed. "You know, I believe Dracula must really have been Italian. No one from Transylvania could be that sexy."

Twenty minutes later, Sabrina was showered, dressed in her faded green and white striped pajamas, and had slipped between the sheets of her twin bed. It had been a mad, bizarre evening and she felt totally drained.

How stupid to let the thought of Alex Ben Raschid upset her so. She had enough problems and responsibilities in her life without worrying about some wealthy playboy's arrogant threats. It was a matter of simple chemistry that had caused those violent reactions to zing between them. What else could it be? She was a young, healthy female with all the usual reactions to a man of Ben Raschid's potent appeal. As far as his own rather excessive attraction was concerned, it was probably the result of the unusual circumstances of their first meeting. According to the columns he was seldom without a woman in his bed, and it was obvious he wasn't used to resistance on the part of the opposite sex. Another pretty face was bound to come along at any moment and she'd be forgotten. Worrying about the man was ridiculous!

"Bree, can I sleep with you tonight?"

She looked up with a weary sigh, which she quickly smothered when she saw David's wistful expression as he stood hesitantly in the doorway. He was so beautiful in that navy Houston Astro T-shirt, she thought tenderly. His sapphire eyes were brilliant against his glowingly healthy tan, and the shining, white blond of his sunstreaked hair, pulled back in the shoulder-length braid Angelina abhorred, only enhanced his strong, classical bone structure.

"Did you watch that horror movie with Angelina?" Sabrina asked, trying to frown. "You know Dr. Swanson told you to stay away from that sort of thing."

He shook his head, a trace of indignation on his face. "I was reading some of Gino's horticulture magazines all evening." He smiled coaxingly. "I'm just lonely. You've been gone all evening, Bree."

She held out for a full two minutes before she melted as she usually did. "All right. Get on your pajamas and brush your teeth." She frowned. "But no talking to the wee hours. You have to get up early and go out on that job in Baytown tomorrow."

He was already turning away. "I won't," he promised eagerly. "I'll go get Miranda."

Which one was Miranda, Sabrina wondered in amusement, as she plumped up the pillow and propped herself up in bed.

Miranda proved to be an extremely wilted-looking daffodil in a natural clay pot. David put the plant carefully on the bedside table between the twin beds and sat down on the other bed with a contented smile. As usual he'd put on the bottoms of the blue cotton pajamas but his bronze, muscular chest with its golden mat of hair was bare. A child in a man's body.

"You don't mind if I leave a light on, do you?" he asked, his worried gaze on the daffodil. "Miranda needs all the light and sunshine we can give her."

And so did he, Sabrina thought, her throat suddenly tight and aching. During those first months when he'd started coming back from a near catatonic state, he'd been plagued by hideous nightmares which had almost ripped him apart. Even now he never slept without at least a night light burning. But she wouldn't think about that. It was over now, and David was so much better.

"Are you going to be able to save her?" she asked gently.

"I think so," David said. "She's responding more every day. All she needs is to know that someone cares what happens to her." His face was grave. "We do care, Miranda," he told the plant earnestly.

"Get into bed and cover up," Sabrina said over the lump in her throat. "Miranda knows you care."

He obediently slipped between the sheets but turned to face her, his deep blue eyes sparkling and wide-awake as ever. There was an almost bell-like radiance about him now, Sabrina thought. It was difficult to believe that he was a year older than she. The mind-expansion drugs, that had robbed him of so much, seemed to have stopped time for him, giving him a childlike simplicity and inner beauty that was poignantly touching.

His gaze was once more on his Miranda. "I think she does know we care now," he said contentedly. Then a tiny frown creased his forehead. "Flowers are so much easier than people, Bree."

"Are they, love?" Sabrina asked.

He nodded. "You can tell when someone is closing up and dying inside just by looking at them, but they won't let you help them. They won't let you near enough to tell them that you care." He bit his lip. "Or maybe I just don't know how. Did I know how before, Bree?" Lately he'd become aware of that time before, but he seemed to regard it almost as another incarnation.

Sabrina shook her head. "You were always too preoccupied to notice before," she answered.

His glance was startled. "But how could I miss it?" he asked incredulously. "It's right there."

"In many ways you see much more clearly now, David."

He shook his head wonderingly as his glance returned once more to his daffodil. There was a moment of silence and when David spoke again his voice was soft. "Bree, do you remember the movie *E.T.*?"

How could she help it, Sabrina thought ruefully. It was David's favorite movie and she had sat through it with him innumerable times. Something about that mythical tale of love and magic had struck an answering chord in the child that he was now.

"Yes, I remember."

"I was thinking," he said dreamily. "do you remember when E.T. touched those flowers and they blossomed and came to life? Wasn't that beautiful?"

"Yes, very beautiful."

His hand reached out and caressed one of Miranda's golden petals with a tender finger. "Wouldn't it be wonderful if we could just reach out to each other like that. Just one touch and we'd all bloom and unfold our petals in the sun. Wouldn't that be wonderful?"

"So wonderful," Sabrina murmured, blinking back tears.

He was still looking at the daffodil, his face absorbed. "Of course, it wouldn't be necessary all the time," he said gravely. "Some people blossom naturally all by themselves." His thoughtful gaze moved to Sabrina's face. "You did, Bree. You're like a poinsettia, all brilliant color and soft velvet petals." He smiled gently. "You're like velvet on the inside too. Sometimes I can feel that softness wrapping around me, keeping me safe and warm." He said simply, "It's nice, Bree."

Sabrina cleared her throat, smiling mistily. "I'm not sure I like you comparing me to such a fragile flower," she said lightly. "They seem to live such a short time."

David frowned. "They're quite strong, really,"

he said earnestly. "They go dormant, you know. They gather strength from the darkness and soon they bloom again."

Strength from the darkness. Yes, she'd discovered in these last two years that she had strength and determination to tap. Pray God, though, that darkness never returned.

"Well, I'm glad you recognize that I have a little stamina," she said briskly. "Now, what did you promise me about going to sleep right away?"

She scooted down in the bed, plumped her pillow, and closed her eyes decisively. She heard David's disappointed sigh and the sounds of him settling down in his own bed. She could hear his light breathing and the restless thrashing as he moved about. Then there was another long silence and she dared a surreptitious peek at him.

He was still wide-awake, his bright blue eyes intent once more on his yellow daffodil. As she watched, his finger reached out again to stroke Miranda's golden petals with loving delicacy. His soft murmur was a mere breath but it was enough to bring the tears to Sabrina's eyes.

"Wonderful."

Three

Sabrina fell to her knees in the obeisance that signaled the end of her performance and looked up at her red-faced client with a cheerful grin. "Congratulations on your promotion, Mr. Selkirk. I'm sure you'll make a fine vice-president."

There was a burst of good-natured laughter from the men at the table as well as scattered applause from the other luncheon patrons of the popular French restaurant. The flustered executive muttered something under his breath that might have been an acknowledgment, but he was too busy handling the jests from his business associates to really comprehend her words.

It was no more than she expected and she rose lightly to her feet and turned away with a friendly wave of her hand. She walked quickly to where Hector Ramirez was waiting at a table by the door. He picked up the portable tape recorder and handed her white velvet cloak to her. "I'll keep a careful watch on this tape, Sabrina, since it's the backup one. Never known you to leave your tape." When she glowered, he said quickly, "It went off pretty well, didn't it? The waiters were fairly cooperative this time. I didn't have to glower threateningly at more than two of them to keep them out of your way while you were performing."

It seldom took more than that ferocious scowl from a man of Hector's bulk to intimidate even the most confident individual. Which was the primary reason Joel had assigned the college student to accompany Sabrina on her jobs. In the gaudy red turban and white, flowing robe he resembled a picturesque harem guard.

"Can I drop you back at the office to pick up your motorcycle?" Sabrina offered, as she put on her ballet slippers.

Hector shook his head. "I've got a term paper to finish. I'll hop a bus to the library, and then hitch a ride with one of my fraternity brothers later and pick it up." He put his big hand solicitously under her elbow as they walked briskly from the restaurant to the parking lot. "As soon as I see you safely to that heap you call a car."

"My Volkswagen's a good deal safer than that cycle of yours," she said dryly. "At least it has four metal walls around it."

"You have no spirit of adventure," Hector scoffed. "You haven't lived until you—" He broke off suddenly with a low, admiring whistle. "Speaking of adventure, will you get a load of that Lamborghini? Driving one of those babies is what I'd call the ultimate experience."

These men and their passion for machinery, Sabrina thought with amusement. First the taxi driver last night and now Hector. She cast a casual glance in the direction he was indicating and suddenly all amusement was wiped from her face.

Alex Ben Raschid, in dark jeans and a black sport shirt, straightened slowly from the fender of the white Lamborghini, looking as supple and dangerous as a panther. The slanting rays of the afternoon sun touched his head, and his dark hair shone with peltlike luster.

"I've been waiting for you," he said curtly, opening the passenger door. "Get in."

"I beg your pardon," Sabrina said blankly. She'd felt a trifle bemused from the surprise of seeing him, but this command immediately caused her to bristle.

"I said, get in," he repeated, his expression grim. "Unless you want me to give everyone in the parking lot an even better show than the one you gave for those lecherous bastards inside."

Ramirez tensed, his eyes narrowed on Ben Raschid's stormy face. "You know this guy, Sabrina?"

"Slightly." Sabrina shrugged. "We met last night at the party in River Oaks. This is Alex Ben Raschid, Hector. Hector Ramirez is my co-worker, Mr. Ben Raschid."

"I knew I should have gone with you on that gig." Hector scowled. "This bozo give you any trouble, Sabrina?"

"You know Princess Rubinoff specified I handle the assignment by myself," Sabrina said, her gaze on Ben Raschid's furious expression. Something had put him in an awesomely bad temper and it was clear Hector's aggressive protectiveness was only serving to aggravate it. "He was no problem. I handled him."

He didn't like that either, Sabrina thought, her lips curving in slightly malicious amusement. Well, what could he expect when he was acting as if she were some little slave girl panting to amuse the great man.

"Get in the car, Sabrina," he said softly, and there was menace beneath the velvet. "Let's see how you manage to handle me today."

"She doesn't have to go anywhere with you," Ramirez said, his jaw jutting out belligerently. "Now, why don't you just buzz off, buster."

"Oh, she has to go with me all right," Ben Raschid said quietly. "That is, if she wants *you* to stay in one piece. It may be the only thing that will save you. At the moment I'm not even sure about that."

Sabrina started to smile at this outrageous threat but her amusement faltered and then faded entirely as her eyes met those of Ben Raschid. This was no playboy's idle boast. There was something coolly competent and extremely lethal about the man. She moved toward the open door of the Lamborghini almost involuntarily.

"It's not worth arguing about. Mr. Ben Raschid will take me home, Hector, and I'll pick up my car later. Will you call Angelina for me and ask her to look in on David if I'm a little late?"

Hector frowned. "You're sure, Sabrina?"

"I'm sure," she said, giving him a reassuring smile as she got in the sports car. "Don't worry, everything will be fine." She cast Ben Raschid a poisonous glance. "The gentleman isn't quite the uncivilized savage he appears."

"Don't bet on it," Ben Raschid snapped, slamming the door and striding around to the driver's seat. A moment later they were roaring out of the parking lot while Hector gazed after them with a troubled expression on his face.

"Your David appears to be very complacent," Ben Raschid said harshly. "I was under the impression that he wouldn't take kindly to your seeing other men. Or does this Angelina offer him her own brand of comfort when you decide to amuse yourself? I understand *ménages à trois* are becoming increasingly popular these days."

Sabrina had forgotten Donahue's misinterpretation of the relationship between David and herself, but evidently he'd given a full report to Ben Raschid. "That's really none of your business," she said sarcastically. "But I'm afraid I've not reached quite your level of sophistication. I find a one-on-one relationship much more desirable."

"I'm glad to hear it," Ben Raschid said, "because that's what I have in mind for you. So you can just resign yourself to giving this Bradford his walking papers. I've never wanted a woman this way before, and you're not getting away from me." He smiled with lazy sensuality. "I promise that once I get you into my bed, you won't want to."

"The great lover," Sabrina scoffed, to hide the breathlessness that flooded her at the thought of Ben Raschid touching her.

"Exactly," he said coolly. "You won't be disappointed. I think you'll find I have enough experience to make you forget your roommate."

The biting acid of his last remark revealed a bitterness that pleased Sabrina. He evidently didn't like the idea of another man receiving favors that were denied him, and she felt a perverse thrill at disconcerting the arrogant Alex Ben Raschid. Her intention of telling him the truth of her relationship was discarded. Once he was convinced that she wouldn't have an affair with him, her deception wouldn't matter. Besides, she had an uneasy feeling she might need all the barricades she could erect between them.

"David loves me," she said truthfully.

"Love is a word for children," Alex said. "I'll teach you more interesting emotions, Sabrina."

"Like lust?"

Ben Raschid smiled intimately, his eyes lingering on her lips. "I had that in mind for lesson one," he admitted.

"I prefer the old-fashioned concepts, like love, affection, and loyalty. I wouldn't be a very good pupil," she said tartly.

"An interesting paradox," Alex said, his lips curving mockingly. "Old-fashioned ideals and a swinging lifestyle. Don't you have trouble reconciling the two?"

"Not at all," she answered coolly. "And now that you understand that our views are incompatible, don't you think you'd better drive me back to pick up my car?"

"Without trying to change your mind?" He shook his head. "I don't give up that easily. You're going to have dinner with me. I intend to show you what a harmless, uncomplicated man I really am."

Sabrina eyed him skeptically. He was about as harmless as a live electric wire and as uncomplicated as a master computer. She noticed that they'd now turned onto the Gulf Freeway and were headed rapidly east toward the Gulf of Mexico. "May I ask where you're taking me?" she asked suspiciously. "You do realize that you've practically kidnapped me? Don't you ever ask instead of take, Mr. Ben Raschid?"

"Alex," he corrected impatiently. "And you'll find I can ask as politely as the next man." He gave her a sly, sideways glance and suddenly a mischievous grin lit the darkness of his face. "If I'm sure the answer will be yes."

Sabrina shook her head, a reluctant smile tugging at the corners of her mouth. "Where are we going?" she persisted.

"Galveston," he answered. "I thought that since neither of us is dressed for dinner, we'd have a picnic on the beach."

"I wouldn't have thought that would be your scene," she said flippantly. "It seems a bit primitive for a sophisticated man of the world."

The glance that he gave her was as intimate as a kiss. His eyes ran over her face and then her body as if he wanted to memorize them. "You persist in underestimating me, Sabrina," he said softly. "I'm very adaptable. You'll find that I can be very primitive."

Sudden color flooded her face and her breath caught in her throat. What on earth was the matter with her? One smoky glance from those dark, guarded eyes and she was trembling like a schoolgirl. Her glance slid quickly away from his. "How did you know where to find me?" she asked, moistening her lips nervously.

"I had Clancy call Noveltygrams and track you down," he answered. He frowned fiercely. "You really do perform that glorified hootchy-kootchy two and three times a day. I couldn't believe it when I walked into that restaurant and saw you dancing for those drooling old goats." His hands tightened on the steering wheel until the knuckles showed white. "It made me sick to my stomach. I had to get out of there or I'd have yanked you out of the place by that gorgeous red hair."

"You could have tried," Sabrina said tartly, her eyes flashing. "My dance is *not* a hootchy-kootchy, and I'd have thought that anyone from a mideastern country such as Sedikhan would appreciate that fact."

"All right, it's a beautiful dance." He glared at her moodily. "And you're so damn beautiful doing it that it makes me ache just watching you. That doesn't mean it's not as provocative as hell. You can't deny that every man in the room was only thinking of one thing while you were moving those hips like some blasted fertility goddess."

"Not everyone has his mind in the bedroom constantly the way you do," Sabrina defended. "It was a joke, for heaven's sake. Those men were just having a good time."

"Well, from now on they can have it without panting after you as if you were a bitch in heat," he said tersely. "I'm not about to let you keep on putting me through this hell."

Her mouth fell open in stunned surprise. The sheer unadulterated nerve of the man! "You have absolutely nothing to say about either my professional or private life," she said icily. "I'll thank you to remember that fact."

The look he threw her was compounded equally of anger and exasperation. Then he drew a deep breath. "Look, I have no intention of quarreling with you. That's not what I had in mind when I was lying awake all night thinking about you. You caught me off guard in the library last night and I knew damn well that I was saying and doing all the wrong things. You needn't be afraid I'm going to throw you down and rape you. I don't operate that way."

He wouldn't need to, not with his virile solar power that could melt all resistance like hot wax. "Then you'll turn the car around and take me back?" she asked.

He scowled. "I didn't say that. Why can't you just relax and try to enjoy yourself. Who knows—by the time the evening is over you might discover I'm not such a bastard after all."

"Do I have a choice?"

"None," he replied. "So we might as well declare a truce." He raised a mocking brow. "Okay?"

"Okay." She sighed, resigned. As he'd said she had little choice, and in a few hours she would be safely back in her apartment. It was a limited commitment at best.

"Good," Alex said. He turned left at Stewart Beach and proceeded away from the crowded bathing area until they came to a deserted stretch of sand a few miles down the road. Then he switched off the engine and turned to face Sabrina. His eyes traveled over her again with the same smoldering intimacy that had been there before. "Now what were you saying back at the restaurant about the way you handled me?"

Sabrina backed against the car door, her green eyes startled as she realized how very isolated they were on this barren stretch of beach. Alex's eyes suddenly gleamed with mischief as he opened his door and got out. He stretched lazily, the movement pulling his dark shirt taut over his lithe muscles.

"Get out, Sabrina," he ordered dryly. "The only appetite I'm about to satisfy at the moment is for the food in the hamper in the trunk."

She got out of the car hurriedly, feeling foolish about having risen to the bait so easily. She helped him spread a beach blanket and tablecloth, and then set out the veritable feast the basket containing: Fried chicken, potato salad, bread, fresh strawberries, and a bottle of red wine.

"Primitive?" She raised an eyebrow quizzically.

He grinned. "I like to live well. Who said picnics have to be hot dogs and marshmallows?"

"Who, indeed," Sabrina said wryly, biting into a crisp piece of chicken.

The silence between them was strangely compatible as they sat cross-legged on the blanket, eating the delicious food with only an occasional remark. Perhaps it was the serenity evoked by the soft sea breeze that induced the lazy euphoria, or the sound of the surf, or the sun setting in a blaze of color. Alex filled their wine glasses and they sat quietly watching the last traces of scarlet fade from the sky, their reflection turning the clouds the delicate pink of cotton candy.

Sabrina leaned back on one elbow with a sigh of contentment. "Will you answer a rather personal question?" she asked hesitantly, thinking dreamily how the fading light hollowed his cheekbones and highlighted that sensual mouth, rather like an El Greco painting. "There's something I've been curious about for the past six months. It's driving me crazy."

His lips twisted mockingly. "We wouldn't want that. There's only one way I want to drive you insane and it's not with curiosity. Ask away."

"The message that Honey told me to give you after my dance. What was the promise that she said she'd kept?"

"You," he said simply, and then began to chuckle at her blank look of surprise. "It's a long story and much too involved to go into at the moment. To put it as briefly as possible, I've always had a passion for redheads and a few years ago Honey made me a pledge. I'd just had an encounter with a very unprincipled redhead, and Honey promised someday she'd find me a redhead I could trust."

"And that's supposed to be me?" Sabrina asked dazedly.

Alex nodded. "You must have made a very deep impression on Honey. Clancy said you became good friends that week they were here in Houston."

Sabrina's lips curved in a reminiscent smile. "We had an instant rapport, and by the time they had to leave we were almost as close as sisters. I'm glad she thought I was worthy of trust."

"Honey is exceptionally naïve. She trusts everyone until they prove her wrong."

"Then you must never have disappointed her," Sabrina said quietly. "She's very fond of you, you know."

His brows lifted in surprise. "You discussed me?"

"Not really. I can only remember one thing she actually said about you in that entire week."

"And that was?"

"Honey said, 'If I were blind and Alex took my hand, I'd trust him to lead me through hell.' "

For a moment there was blank surprise on that closed, usually cynical-looking face. Then to Sabrina's amazement a surge of color flooded his bronze cheeks and his dark eyes were suddenly naked and vulnerable. He hurriedly glanced away and his voice was curiously husky when he spoke. "As I said, Honey's incredibly naïve, but she's right in this instance. I'd do a hell of a lot for her. And there aren't many people in this world worthy of affection."

"What a very cynical thing to say! And how completely untrue. The world is full of people who deserve all the affection we can give them. Surely you must have found that. What about your parents? Aren't you close to them?"

"Not exactly." The words were oddly stilted. "I haven't seen very much of them since I was a small child."

Sabrina's eyes widened in surprise. "I don't understand." Surely even if Alex came from a broken home, he would be close to one of his parents. "Are they divorced?"

"No, they're still together." He laughed shortly. "Of course, that might be due to my grandfather's distaste for divorce. They wouldn't have wanted to give up what they'd gained by selling me to him."

"*Selling you?*"

"My parents find Sedikhan a trifle barbaric compared to the more civilized pleasures of the Riviera." Alex's tone was mocking, but his expression was bitter. "When I was eight, they signed over complete custody of me to my grandfather in return for a villa in Cannes and a very generous lifetime income."

"And they told you what they'd done?" Sabrina asked, appalled.

He shook his head. "My grandfather showed me the contract," he said. His eyes flicked from the rolling surf to her horrified face and for an instant there was something hurt and lost in the depths of them. Then it was gone, masked by a fierce defensiveness. "I'm glad he did it. It was better that I realized at once I couldn't rely on them just because they were my parents. I would have found out later anyway. The parasites of the world always reveal themselves eventually. Sometimes you just have to wait a little longer for the clever ones to show their true colors."

"My God, you were only eight years old," Sabrina said faintly, feeling a little sick to her stomach. "Surely he might have waited until you were older." Could anyone blame Alex for his lack of trust in his fellow man with the kind of upbringing those few poignant sentences had revealed?

"Why should he have?" Alex asked simply. "My grandfather's a great one for calling a spade a spade. He didn't do it to hurt me. I think he genuinely cares for me in his own way. He just wanted to protect me from any possibility of my parents using me later."

"And did they try to use you later?" she asked gently, hoping against hope he'd answer in the negative.

"Of course," he said with a curiously bitter-sweet smile. "I told you, parasites always react according to their natures. I was fortunate that my grandfather had prepared me for it."

"Yes, very fortunate," Sabrina said huskily, her throat tight with tears as she thought of that vulnerable little boy taught so early about pain and disillusion.

"I didn't need them anyway," he said defiantly. "I had my cousin, Lance, and my grandfather. I didn't need anyone else."

"No, I can see that," Sabrina said lightly, glancing hurriedly away so that he wouldn't see the sudden mist of tears in her eyes. "You wouldn't need anyone but them."

Alex shook his head impatiently. "My God, why am I telling you all this? I don't think I've even given my charming parents a thought in the last five years and you have me spilling out my entire past history. It all happened a long time ago. None of it matters now."

But it did matter. Sabrina had caught a glimpse of another Alex Ben Raschid entirely in the past few minutes, an Alex capable of loyalty and affection and as vulnerable to hurt as any other man. She'd been unbearably moved by that brief insight, and found herself wanting to reach out and hold him close as she did David after one of his nightmares.

"Just because your parents hurt you doesn't mean that no one else can be trusted, Alex," she said gently.

"They didn't hurt me," he denied fiercely, and already the mockery was beginning to mask that instant of vulnerability. "And of course *you* can be trusted, Sabrina. Honey would never have sent you if you couldn't, would she?"

"No, she wouldn't," Sabrina agreed quietly. Why did the sudden raising of that barrier of mockery cause this aching pain in her breast?

Alex's expression darkened moodily. "She apparently didn't delve too deeply into your personal life. I don't know how the hell she expected me to trust you when you're already playing house with another man." His resentful eyes traveled over her scantily clad form in the midnight blue harem outfit. "Not to mention the kick you seem to get out of giving every man in Houston his quota of cheap thrills."

It seemed the truce had definitely come to an end. Sabrina carefully put her wine glass down on the sand and said quietly. "I don't have to take that from you. I think it's time you drove me home."

Alex muttered a very explicit curse. "Why do I always say the wrong things to you?" he asked in exasperation. "At this point I should be wooing you gently. Why does everything have to be different with you?"

"We're obviously incompatible. That's what I've been trying to tell you. Not only are our lifestyles as far apart as the poles but we have different attitudes and commitments."

"Commitment." He repeated the word as if it left a nasty taste in his mouth. "You consider that you have some type of commitment to this David of yours?"

Her eyes met his directly. "Yes," she said candidly. "There's no question of my commitment to David." A look of wonder in sapphire eyes, a tender finger stroking velvet petals. David.

"Commitments can be broken," he said tightly, his dark eyes smoldering. "It seems I'll just have to convince you how desirable it would be to make that break. Honey can be fooled like any other woman. I probably can't trust you any more than I can anyone else." His expression darkened broodingly. "But who the hell cares?"

Then suddenly he was pushing her down on the blanket, leaning over her, a hand on each side of her face but not touching, his body heat tantalizing her. She felt as though his dark eyes were hypnotizing her, holding her in a web of golden languor. Then his lips were covering hers—not roughly, but with infinitely gentle butterfly kisses that teased until her mouth instinctively shaped itself to take more. She could feel the shudder that shook him as she arched against the warmth of his body, slipping her arms slowly over his shoulders and around his neck to bury her fingers in his hair.

Then his tongue was teasing her lips provocatively, tracing the pouting line erotically. "Open your mouth," he said hoarsely. "Let me love you, Sabrina."

She shook her head dazedly, her senses swimming from his experienced lovemaking, but he took the gesture of bewilderment for negation. "Don't say no, Sabrina." He framed her cheeks with his hands. "You won't be sorry. It will be good for you." Then his lips were hard on hers, not coaxing, but taking now, parting her lips almost savagely to deepen the kiss excitingly. He groaned deep in his throat and suddenly the body he had withheld from her was joined to hers in a breathless embrace.

Alex's arms chained her to his muscular form, rolling her over so they lay side by side on the blanket. His lips probed hers in hot, drugging kisses that left her aware of nothing but a nameless hunger. His mouth moved from hers to bite gently on the sensitive cord of her neck, then down to the fullness of her breasts, lingering on the golden flesh of her cleavage before his hands moved slowly to unfasten the chiffon top. Instinctively her hands rose to stop him. It was all happening too fast. Alex's eyes were glazed with passion as they glanced up impatiently to meet her own. He took her lips again, slowly, sensuously, sending her into a world of erotic sensation. She could feel the muscles of his thighs go taut as his hands cupped her breasts, teasing the peaks through the thin material. She gasped, the muscles of her stomach tensing, her breasts swelling at the stimulation that was causing a fluid melting in every limb.

"You're beautiful, do you know that?" he muttered, his lips parting from hers briefly, only to dip down to taste again and again the honey of her lips in hot, scorching kisses. "When you were dancing, all I could think of was getting you alone so I could have all that beauty to myself. I want to see you, every lovely inch of you." His gaze still holding hers, his hands moved deliberately to the front fastening of the midriff.

Sabrina didn't try to stop him this time. She knew with a rush of primitive pride that she wanted him to look at her and find her desirable. He carefully parted the flimsy chiffon barrier and gazed down at her, his eyes dark and intent. He was absolutely still for a moment, before he made a low sound of mindless hunger and lowered his lips to caress the taut, rosy peaks. She arched convulsively as his hands cupped her naked breasts that his burning mouth was caressing.

She gave a little cry that was half protest, half plea. "No, please, Alex." She was on fire, yet feeding on the flame, writhing captive of a response she'd never experienced. Pleading with him to stop, knowing that if he did she would hate him for withdrawing this exquisite torment of the senses.

With easy strength he rolled over until she was on top of him, their bodies fitting together with unbelievable intimacy. His lips covered hers in a long, hot joining while one hand held her hips glued to his thrusting body, and the other caressed her naked back. As their lips parted, he buried his mouth in the hollow of her throat. "God, I'm aching for you. I've been in a fever for you, Sabrina. You've got to belong to me."

She couldn't answer. What had seemed impossible a few hours ago was now happening. She lowered her lips to his with a sense of inevitability, a moth to the flame he'd fired so skillfully. She kissed him with a sweet responsiveness that may have lacked Alex's experience but evidently was more than satisfying, to judge by the shudder that wracked his body.

His arms tightened around her convulsively for a moment, then with a muttered imprecation he rolled over abruptly and tore himself away from her. She lay where he had left her, staring at him in hurt bewilderment. Her body suddenly chilled when separated from his warmth.

He sat a few feet away, his arms clasping his knees, his body rigid. He fumbled in his shirt pocket for a slender brown cigarette, lighting it with a shaking hand and inhaling deeply. He glanced at her. "Please cover up," he said, his eyes fixed compulsively on her bare breasts. "I'm trying my damndest to keep my hands off you."

Sabrina's hands flew to the front of her midriff, his sarcasm making her feel suddenly cheap. She sat up, fighting tears, fumbling at the fastening of the chiffon top.

"Wait." He was kneeling beside her. With urgent hands he parted the midriff and gazed for a long moment. Then, lowering his head, he kissed each taut peak lingeringly. "I didn't mean to be so sharp, sweetheart. It's just that I'm aching for you."

Sabrina drew a shaky breath, leaning toward him yearningly.

He drew back slowly. "You're so damn lovely," he said roughly. He pulled the top closed reluctantly, fastening it slowly. Then he took her in his arms as carefully as if she were a beloved child and rocked her soothingly. "And so very much *mine*. I've never felt so close to anyone in my entire life. It scares the hell out of me, love."

She buried her face in his shoulder, her arms slipping around his waist very naturally. She'd been subjected to so many tumultuous and bewildering emotions with him that she gratefully accepted the comfort he was extending. "You don't want to make love to me any more?" she asked wonderingly. It seemed impossible that he could stop so abruptly when she was still aching and throbbing for more.

He laughed shortly, his hands stroking her silky hair gently. "Oh yes, I want to make love to you. I came within an inch of taking you on this damn blanket."

"Then, why . . ." Her voice trailed off as some fugitive feeling of shame overtook her. Was she so lost in his sensual web that she would plead for him to make love to her? The thought sent a shock of distaste through her, dispelling the euphoric mood generated by the wine and his sexual expertise. She stiffened in his arms and tried to draw back, but at the first signs of withdrawal he bound her tighter to him with instinctive possessiveness.

"I've got an idea we're going to be something special together," he said thickly. "I didn't want to start our relationship like some sex-starved adolescent at a drive-in movie. When I get you into bed, I may not let you out for a week, so we'd better be comfortable."

He kissed her quickly and then reluctantly let her go. He bent to bundle the blanket and hamper into a careless pile, then stowed them in the trunk of the car. In a matter of minutes they were traveling the streets of Galveston. Alex didn't speak until they'd left the outskirts of the port city and were speeding down the Gulf Freeway toward Houston.

"You're coming home with me tonight," he told her quietly. "I'll take you back to your place to pick up your clothes. You won't have to bring much, just enough to last until I can buy you others."

"I can't do that!" Sabrina cried, shocked out of the dazed bemusement his lovemaking had woven about her.

Alex's mouth hardened ruthlessly. "If you think I'm going to let you spend another night with that lover of yours, you're mistaken," he said, his hands tightening on the steering wheel until his knuckles whitened. "I'm going to own you completely, Sabrina, and if anyone so much as touches you, I'll destroy him."

There was an implacable sincerity in his voice. Sabrina shivered uncontrollably at the picture his words evoked. She knew she could never live the life he'd planned for her even to repeat the exquisite sensual pleasure he'd shown her. After the freedom she'd known all her life, the role of a rich man's possession would stifle her. Even if there hadn't been her responsibility toward David, the situation would have been impossible.

"For how long?" she asked bitterly. "Until the next curvy body catches your eye?"

"Do you want me to say forever?" he asked. "I don't believe in forever." He reached over and caressed her thigh. "Will it satisfy you to know that I can't imagine anyone else in my bed? And that this is the first time in my life I've felt that way?"

She pulled her leg away from his touch, liking it far too much. "It wouldn't work," Sabrina said shakily. "You'd soon get bored with me. I'm not terribly brilliant or fabulously talented. I'm probably not even the prettiest girl you've known."

"No, you're not," he said coolly. "You're intelligent, but no Einstein, and I've known many women who were more classically beautiful." He grinned mischievously. "I'll have to judge your other 'talents' later." Then he sobered. "I won't be bored with you, Sabrina. You fit me. I enjoy your spirit and independence, and you have a bright, clear-thinking mind."

"So it's my brain that attracts you?" she scoffed.

"No," he admitted, "that's only a plus." His dark eyes ran over her lingeringly. "There's a sexual chemistry between us that's stronger than any I've ever known. I find you infinitely desirable. You can turn me on more by tilting your head or wrinkling that aristocratic little nose than any other woman can by doing a striptease. I want you to know that I've never kept a woman before. I'm not saying there haven't been plenty of women. I'm no celibate. I take what's offered, but I've never wanted the responsibility of a permanent mistress. I've always found it easy enough to satisfy my physical needs without the demands of that type of relationship."

"Then why start now?" Sabrina asked coldly, imagining with a twinge of hot anger the many women who'd appeased those needs.

"Trust a woman to misunderstand," he growled. "I'm trying to tell you that I think of you differently. For the first time in my life I want a woman totally dependent on me. I want to buy your clothes, pay your bills. I want everything you have to come from me."

"That's pretty chauvinistic, isn't it?" she asked caustically. "I'm a person in my own right, not some kind of robot programmed for your pleasure."

"I don't want a robot, Sabrina. I want a warm, responsive woman in my arms."

They'd arrived at the apartment complex and Alex drove unerringly to her apartment area and parked smoothly. She didn't remind him about her car. She only wanted the security of home now. After switching off the engine, he turned to her. He pulled her close and buried his face in her hair. "God, you're good to hold. I've been wanting to touch you since we left the beach." His mouth covered hers urgently, as if he were starved for the taste of her. Sabrina melted against him, forgetting everything but the potent magic he stirred in her. "I needed that," he groaned hoarsely, when their lips finally parted. "I can't take much more of this." He pushed her away, and ran his hand through his hair. "I'll give you forty-five minutes. If you're not down here by that time, I'm coming up to get you."

She gazed up at him, tears misting her emerald eyes. Her gaze lingered yearningly on the bold, cynical features she probably wouldn't see again after tonight. She'd do all she could to further that aim, out of sheer self-preservation. Alex had reached out and touched her, and not only on a physical level. That other, more ephemeral, closeness could be infinitely more dangerous to her. "You really expect me to do it, don't you?" she asked wonderingly. "Disrupt my life, give up my friends, turn myself into some sort of plaything for your gratification."

"Don't be a fool, Sabrina," he said, frowning. "I could have taken you on that beach tonight and you wouldn't have done a thing to stop me. You want me as much as I want you. Do you think I can't feel it when you're in my arms?"

"No, I must be pretty obvious," she said simply. "I don't have your breadth of experience, and I can't hide, or connive, or mask my feelings. I wanted you to make love to me and I couldn't have stopped as you did. If you hadn't stopped, perhaps I'd be committed to you in a way that would make you uncomfortable."

She backed away from him, pressing against the door as he reached for her. "No, don't touch me!" She shook her head desperately. "You did stop, so we're both saved. Believe me, I don't want to feel any sort of commitment to a man like you. It would destroy me. There's no room for you in my life. Stay out of it, Alex!"

"You're not going back to him," he said harshly, his dark eyes blazing. "You belong to me!"

Sabrina wrenched her arm away and jumped out of the car. She turned, her breasts heaving, her flaming hair wild about her pale face. "I belong to myself! I won't be owned or pampered or made into something I'm not. I won't be your mistress, Alex." She turned and stalked away.

His voice followed her with soft intensity. "You will, Sabrina, I promise you. You will."

Angelina was sitting on the couch in front of the television set but she looked up with a sigh of relief as Sabrina came into the apartment. She leaned forward to flick off the set. "I'm glad you're home," she said, her plump face concerned. "When Hector phoned, he was yammering something about Lamborghinis and over-sexed bozos. I couldn't make heads or tails out of it." Her gaze narrowed on Sabrina's flushed face and suspiciously bright eyes. "Are you all right?"

"I'm fine," Sabrina said throatily, shrugging out of her cape. "David wasn't worried, was he?"

"I just told him you were working late." She stood up and straightened her flowered overblouse. "He's downstairs in our apartment with Gino. They're going to watch that National Geographic special together. I'll send him up to you when it's over."

"Has he had his dinner?"

"Of course he's had his dinner," Angelina said indignantly. "Would I let the boy starve while I had enough lasagna to feed an army?"

"Sorry, I wasn't thinking," Sabrina said, smiling with an effort. "I should have known you'd take good care of him for me. You always do."

"I should think so," Angelina sniffed, as she crossed to the front door. She paused and her face was suddenly serious. "You know that we're always glad to have David at any time, Sabrina. He'll always be safe with us. You can't go on devoting your entire life to him as you've been doing for the past two years. You haven't even had a date since David came out of the hospital." She frowned sternly. "If you want to see this young man again, you do it."

"I won't be seeing him again. There's no way it could work out for us." She smiled sadly. "Besides, he's not the type of man you'd approve of my becoming involved with, Angelina. His intentions are definitely not honorable."

"Neither were my Gino's." She grinned impishly. "For that matter neither were mine." She turned to leave and then suddenly whirled back to face Sabrina. "I forgot to tell you. David's father called this evening while you were out."

"Jess?" Sabrina asked worriedly. "Was he calling from the ranch?" Jess called every Saturday evening with clocklike precision to speak with David. Any deviation from this norm made her definitely uneasy.

Angelina nodded. "He asked you to return his call when you came in."

As the door closed behind Angelina, Sabrina was already moving across the room toward the phone on the end table.

Jess Bradford's deep voice answered at once.

"Jess, this is Sabrina. Is Sue all right?"

"She's fine, Bree," Jess shot back. "I knew you'd jump to conclusions when I called. The doctor says she's doing better than she has for quite a while." There was a long pause. "But she doesn't think she's up to coming to the rodeo this weekend. I thought I'd give you some warning so you could prepare David."

"Oh, Jess, he's going to be so disappointed," Sabrina wailed. "He's worked so hard to get back his old skills. We've been going down to the stable every Saturday for the past seven months. Can't you get her to change her mind?"

"I don't even want to try, Bree," Jess said simply. "I can't risk her losing ground now that she's on her way back. I almost lost both of them when David was hospitalized."

"I know, Jess," Sabrina said, her voice gentle. In many ways, Jess's ordeal had been the worst— Sue's nervous breakdown when she was unable to accept David's problem had literally torn him apart.

"It's not that she doesn't want to see him," Jess went on wearily. "She's begun to talk about him again. Nothing much, just a remark now and then. But at least it's a start."

"Yes, it's a start," Sabrina agreed softly. David had been born when Sue was in her early forties and she'd almost given up hope of having a child. David had seemed a miracle to her, and the bond between them had been one of the strongest and most loving Sabrina had ever known. Yet it hadn't been strong enough for Sue to bear David's tragedy. The only way she'd been able to survive her pain was to close herself away from all thought of David. She hadn't even been permitted to see him since he'd left the hospital.

"I don't think this would be the time for her to see him anyway," Jess said, a thread of anxiety in his voice. "What if he gets hurt in the rodeo while she's there? Are you sure Swanson okayed his entering the competition? The doctor won't even let him drive a car!"

"There are different skills involved," she answered

patiently. "The reason David isn't allowed to drive is the monotony factor. The doctor thinks he might lose concentration and have an accident. It's very difficult not to pay attention when you're on the back of a bucking bronco. You know that David can do anything with horses, Jess."

"I know he *could*," Jess said pointedly. "He's not the same person, Bree. You know that better than anyone."

"That doesn't mean we have to write off everything he was before," she argued passionately. "He can do this, Jess. And by God, I want him to have his chance!"

"Okay, simmer down, Bree," Jess said. "I know you wouldn't let him ride if you thought there was any chance it was unsafe. I was just concerned."

"So am I, Jess," she whispered, closing her eyes. She'd been frightened out of her wits since the moment David had told her he wanted to enter the competition. "But he really wants this. He's been riding in the Houston Rodeo since he was sixteen. We can't keep him in a cocoon forever. He's got to begin to live again."

"I know you're right," Jess said wearily. "It's just so blasted difficult to accept. I guess I just want to take care of him."

"You'll be here on Saturday, then?" Sabrina asked.

"You're damn right," he said gruffly. "Tell him I'll be there with bells on. Juan Mendoza is lending me his box at the Astrodome so we'll practically be in David's lap when he takes home the prize money."

"I'm so glad, Jess," Sabrina said huskily. "He needs all the support we can give him."

"Until Saturday, Bree." He broke the connection with a soft click.

Yes, until Saturday. She replaced the receiver wearily and walked toward her bedroom. This was what was important and real in her life. Not that mad, sensual magic she'd experienced on the beach tonight and certainly not Alex Ben Raschid. That being the case, it made no sense that she was suffering this sudden, aching loneliness. Absolutely no sense at all.

Four

"I told you he could do it, Jess!" Sabrina said jubilantly, her face alight with a fierce pride. She threw herself into his arms, and hugged him ecstatically. "Wasn't he wonderful! Third place! Did you see his face?"

"I was too busy looking at yours," Jess said dryly, unwinding her arms from around his neck. "For a moment there I wasn't sure which one of you had won the prize." Despite his joking words there was a suspicious moisture in Jess's eyes as his gaze tried to search out David's figure in the pens at the far end of the huge arena.

"Oh, it was his prize," she said softly, her emerald eyes glowing like stars. "It was his victory all the way." She sat down on the padded seat in the box and sighed contentedly. Third place! Her glance moved absently around the opaque, domed auditorium, scarcely noticing the gaily dressed western audience in attendance at the Houston Rodeo. She was too filled with exhilaration generated by David's triumph to be conscious of anything else. "Weren't you proud of him, Jess?"

Jess Bradford sat down beside her. "Very proud," he said quietly, taking her hand in his. "As proud as I am of you, Bree. You've worked miracles since he left the hospital two years ago. I don't know what Sue and I would have done if you hadn't been there for him." Jess's gray eyes darkened with pain. "God, it's such a waste. He was so brilliant. Why would he want to experiment with drugs, anyway?"

"Why does anyone?" Sabrina asked soberly. "Curiosity, perhaps. David always wanted to try everything, do everything. If he'd been lucky, he might have satisfied his curiosity and got off scot-free." Her face was taut with pain. "He wasn't lucky. The acid that pusher sold him was very dangerous stuff."

"I wish I could get my hands on that bastard," Jess said grimly. "I'd tear him apart."

"David doesn't even remember him," Sabrina said. Her clasp tightened on Bradford's work-roughened hand. "And I try not to myself. It's over, Jess. All we can do is pick up the pieces."

Jess's rugged face was creased in a frown, his gray eyes brooding. Then his expression brightened slightly. "I didn't tell you, Bree. Sue and I had a long talk last night. She wants you to bring David home for a visit."

"But you said—"

"She believes that it's time," Jess interrupted. "She thinks she can take it now." His face was grave. "I hope to hell she's right."

"So do I," Sabrina said, biting her lip worriedly. "If she's not, it could hurt them both terribly."

"That's why I want you to come with him. You've become the center of his life now, Bree." His gaze was serious. "He may need you. Can you come right away?"

How could she not come when he put it like that? Yet it undoubtedly presented problems. They needed the money she earned at Noveltygrams far too much for her to run the risk of being replaced, as she surely would be if she just blithely took off without clearing it with Joel.

"I'll have to see if I can make arrangements," she said, running her hand distractedly through her hair. "When are you going back to the ranch?"

"Tonight," he said. "I don't want to leave Sue alone too long." He leaned forward and kissed Sabrina gently on the forehead. "Don't worry about it, honey. If you can't work things out, we'll just have to postpone it."

"I'll call you Monday and let you know," Sabrina promised. She looked up and leaned forward eagerly as a blare of trumpets announced the starting of the grand parade. The finale was a colorful parade of all the rodeo participants, led by the country-western superstar who was this year's lead attraction. She applauded enthusiastically at the stirring spectacle, her eyes searching the column of riders. "Do you see David?"

Then she spotted him near the end of the parade. He was dressed in black jeans and a brilliant blue satin shirt, his golden braid gleaming under the lights. He was an almost barbarically handsome figure on his black stallion as he lifted his head, his eyes searching the stands. When he saw them, his face lit with such joy that she caught her breath. He took off his black Stetson and waved it jubilantly at her.

Sabrina waved back, her throat tight and aching with tears. She saw the eagerness on his face as he suddenly gathered the reins, his gaze still fixed on her face. Sabrina suddenly knew what he was going to do. "Oh, no," she whispered. "He wouldn't, would he?"

"He would," Jess said, his lips twitching in amusement.

He did.

He left his position in the parade, cut across

the vast arena in front of the outraged superstar and his entourage, and reined in before their box.

"Hi, Bree," he said happily, his face alight with pride. At a signal, his horse bowed low before Sabrina. "Good trick, isn't it? I wanted it to be a surprise. Every time you had to work and Gino took me to the stables in your place, I practiced it." He looked around in surprise at the applause of the crowd, then grinned delightedly and waved his hat in acknowledgment. He turned back, his expression hopeful. "Did you like it, Bree?"

Sabrina could feel the color stain her cheeks as the eyes of the entire audience turned to their box. Yet all she could say to David was, "I loved it. It's a wonderful trick."

David's pleased smile was rainbow brilliant. He edged the horse closer, then stood in the saddle balancing for a moment before vaulting lightly over the rail into the box.

Oh Lord, what next?

"Did you know that there's an amusement park right next door, Bree?" he asked excitedly, not even noticing the crowd's renewed applause. His face was eager. "Could we go over there after the rodeo?"

Yes, she knew about the amusement park and so had he formerly. How many times had they run over to the park with their friends after a rodeo? "I don't see why not, love," she said lightly, over the lump in her throat. "I want to see if you can ride those merry-go-round horses as well as you did that bronco." She turned, "Jess?"

"It's all right with me," Jess said quietly. "I'll meet you down at the pens and help you curry your horse and stable him temporarily. Bree can meet us at the front entrance."

His face alight with excitement, David nodded and turned back to the rail.

"David."

Sabrina impulsively moved forward. To hell with their amused audience. She kissed him gently on the cheek. "I'm so proud of you."

"I'm glad," he said simply, but his smile could have lit all of Houston. Then he vaulted over the rail and onto the black horse and was riding back to his position in the parade.

"I'll see you in about twenty minutes, Bree," Jess drawled, as he left the box. She nodded absently, her gaze on that proud, glowing figure on the glossy black stallion.

The huge crowd started moving up the stairs of the stadium as the last of the parade left the arena. Sabrina had gathered her belongings from the box and joined the slow crawl to the exits when a firm hand pulled her out of the aisle into the now vacant bleachers.

"Hello again, Miss Courtney," Clancy Donahue said cordially.

His massive figure looked much more at ease in Tony Lama boots, Levi's, and a blue chambray shirt than it had in the tuxedo, and his breezy grin was just as warm.

"You look right at home with all these cowboys, Mr. Donahue," Sabrina said. "Are you here with your family?"

He shook his head. "I've always been a loner," he answered. "I've been too busy batting around the world raising hell to acquire any dependents. Alex and Lance are as close as I've ever come to a family."

"Yes, I remember you mentioned knowing Alex as a boy," Sabrina said. "Was that in Sedikhan?"

"Yep, I was bossing one of old Karim's oil rigs when he was scouting around for someone to take over the job of tutoring the boys."

"Tutoring?" Sabrina's eyes widened in surprise.

A rough diamond like Donahue seemed a bizarre choice of tutor for a boy destined to be one of the wealthiest and most powerful men in the world.

"It came as a shock to me, too," Donahue said dryly. "But the old man knew what he wanted. When he called me into his office, he had a dossier on me that dated back to the time I was in diapers. He knew Alex would have to be tough as steel to survive and keep what was his. Sedikhan isn't exactly the most civilized country, even these days. My job was to make sure he was smarter, and a hell of a lot more lethal, than the wolves who would try to gobble him up."

"And did you succeed?"

Donahue's grin was just as genial but there was a glint in those cool blue eyes like sunlight on a bared sword. "What do you think?" he asked softly.

Sabrina shivered as she remembered the sudden chill she'd known in the parking lot three days ago when Ben Raschid had confronted Hector Ramirez. "I think perhaps you did your job very well, indeed."

"So do I, Miss Courtney," Donahue said with satisfaction. He made a face. "Sometimes I think I did too good a job. A little cynicism goes with the territory, but Alex has problems trusting anyone these days. It's turning him into an exceptionally lonely man."

"It doesn't appear to bother him very much," Sabrina said skeptically. "And according to the gossip columns he has more than enough willing companions."

"Women?" Donahue shook his head. "Alex doesn't have any use for women except in the most basic sense." His eyes narrowed thoughtfully on her face. "At least he didn't until now."

"Me?" She shook her head. "I assure you that

Alex views me in exactly the same light as he does other women."

"Somehow I don't think so, or I wouldn't be here right now, Miss Courtney." He paused. "I have a message for you."

"I gather this meeting isn't accidental."

"Well, in a way it is. Alex didn't know you were here until he spotted you on closed-circuit television."

"Alex is here?" She felt a rush of panic.

Clancy Donahue gestured across the arena. "Sedikhan Oil has a corporate box, and Alex is entertaining a few guests." He raised his eyebrows puckishly. "A mideastern head of state, the mayor, and a few movie stars." He shot her a sidelong glance to judge the effect of his words.

"How nice for him," she said flatly, only half hearing him, wondering wildly how she could escape without seeing Alex.

"He wants you to join us, Sabrina," Donahue said quietly.

"No!" The word burst out with the force of a pistol shot. Then, gaining more control of herself, she lowered her voice. "Please convey my thanks to Alex, but I have other plans."

All the laughter left Donahue's face. "You don't want to defy him this time, Sabrina. He's not in a very good mood. In fact, that's quite an understatement. I hope I never see him as angry as when he saw you kiss that cowboy."

"He saw me kiss David?" she asked faintly.

"Fifty thousand people saw you kiss him," Donahue amended dryly. "But Alex was the only one who broke the stem of his champagne glass when he watched your touching little scene. He got quite a nasty cut, too."

"Perhaps he had too much to drink," she said

coolly. "I'm sure my actions couldn't have such a violent effect on Alex."

"It's none of my business what's been happening between you two, but don't underestimate your effect on Alex. He's been perfect hell to work with the past week and I'd bet the responsibility lies on that little red head of yours," Donahue said grimly. "I also know what I saw in his face upstairs. He said two words to me—'Get her!'—and I knew I'd better not slip up on this little assignment." He smiled coaxingly. "So how about it, Sabrina? You wouldn't want to get me in trouble with Alex would you? Why don't you come along like a good girl?"

"Does he pay you extra for acting as a pimp?"

She thought for a moment that he just might hit her. But he drew a deep breath and the smooth control was back. He said coldly, "I'm not bringing you to his bed, Miss Courtney. Alex wouldn't thank me for that. He likes to stage his own seductions in his own time. I'm just a messenger inviting you to a very respectable party.

That half the society women in Houston would give their eyeteeth to attend," he added ironically.

Sabrina felt a twinge of remorse that her temper had led her into such a harsh condemnation. She couldn't help liking Clancy Donahue and it was true he was doing nothing shameful in carrying out Ben Raschid's orders.

She turned toward him, her eyes glistening with tears. "I'm sorry," she said in a low voice, "that was terribly bitchy of me."

"You're damn right it was," he said grimly, then smiled reluctantly. "But not entirely unjustified. My duties don't usually include standing in for Alex. He would have come after you himself if he weren't tied up with a rather temperamental oil sheik. Mahoud wouldn't understand being deserted for a lowly woman." Then, noticing her tear-brightened eyes, he touched her cheek gently with one finger. "Damn, you're just a baby!" he said abruptly. "Do you want some good advice? Run like hell, kid."

"You're not being a very loyal employee, are you?" Sabrina asked, liking him more every moment.

He said lightly, "I have a hunch you're a great deal more vulnerable than the ladies who inhabit Alex's world. He's pretty potent stuff. He could hurt you badly."

"I know." Her expression was nakedly revealing.

Donahue smiled almost tenderly. "It appears my warning comes a little late."

"I'll get over it," she said determinedly.

"I hope so, Sabrina," he said skeptically, his blue eyes kind. "In the meantime I'd get as far away from Houston as I could. Alex isn't going to let you go easily. Not now."

Sabrina laughed shakily. "This isn't some feudal kingdom; this is one of the most modern cities in the world, and I'm not leaving my home and my friends just because you think Alex may decide to practice some form of sexual harassment. That would be ridiculous." She broke away from him, then turned back abruptly. "I'm not running away," she said softly, "but thank you for your concern. You're a nice person, Clancy Donahue."

"I like you, too, Sabrina, but you're making a mistake." He shrugged. "Now, what do I tell Alex?"

"I don't suppose you could tell him you missed me in the crowd?" she asked hopefully.

Donahue shook his head. "He's probably watching us right now on closed-circuit television."

She shivered at the thought, imagining Alex's eyes on her. It was almost as if he were right here beside them. She lifted her chin defiantly. "Then you can tell him I had a previous engagement," she said, starting up the now deserted stairs. She smiled recklessly. "Tell him I regret refusing his gracious invitation, but I have a date with a carousel."

"Hi, Jean," Sabrina called cheerfully as she entered the modest offices of Noveltygrams Incorporated on Monday morning.

Jean Roberts, Joel's receptionist, looked up with a sunny smile. "Hi, Sabrina. What brings you in? Going to hit the boss for a raise?"

Sabrina shook her head, her ponytail bouncing saucily. "Nope, I wanted a few days off to go visit friends. Will you tell Joel I'm here?"

Jean nodded and picked up the phone, speaking into it briefly. "He says to go right in."

Sabrina nodded, then waved gaily before opening the door to the inner office.

Joel Craigen leaned back in his chair and said genially, "You're looking great, Sabrina." He waved to a chair in front of his desk. "Sit down and tell me what I can do for you."

She perched on the edge of the chair. "I was just wondering, could I have a little time off, Joel?" she asked hesitantly. When he didn't respond immediately, she continued, "If it's inconvenient right now, of course I'll forget about it."

Joel was toying with a pencil, not looking at her. "We might work something out."

"That's great! I'll only be gone for a few days, Joel."

He dropped his pencil on the desk and rubbed hard at his thick neck. "Well, actually, Sabrina, I've been trying to reach you for the last half hour. I wanted to have a little talk with you. The truth is, I've decided to discontinue the bellygrams."

"Discontinue?" she asked blankly. "But they're one of the most popular grams on your list! Jean told me last week there were lots of bookings. You'd have to cancel them!"

"Then I'll cancel them," he said flatly. "The bellygrams are out."

Sabrina shook her head dazedly. It didn't make sense. Why would he cancel one of his most lucrative acts? She smiled uneasily. "Well, if they're out, they're out. Can you fit me into one of the other acts?"

Joel shuffled papers on his desk. "Uh, we're pretty well staffed right now, Sabrina. You know how it is." He looked up at last to meet her disappointed gaze. "Oh, hell!" he exploded in disgust, tossing the papers aside and running his fingers through his thinning hair. "Dammit, Sabrina, this is bull," he said roughly. "You're fired. I can't use you any more. Not now, not ever."

"But why?" she asked, stunned. "I'm good. You know I'm good, and I've always been very reliable. I don't deserve this. What did I do wrong?"

"I wish I knew," he said wearily. "But you sure made someone mad as hell."

"What on earth do you mean? Did one of my clients complain?"

"Not directly. All I know is I got a phone call this morning from Jim Hudson, head of the legal department of Sedikhan Petroleum."

"Sedikhan Petroleum!" Sabrina gasped.

Joel gave her a keen glance. "You know something about this, Sabrina?"

"I may," she answered grimly, her fists clenching involuntarily. "What did they want?"

Craigen took out a cigar and lit it before leaning back again in his chair. He quoted briefly, "Sabrina Courtney is not to perform in any capacity. She is to be terminated immediately, or any required action will be taken against Noveltygrams."

"That's ridiculous," Sabrina said furiously, "What could they possibly do to you?"

"Plenty," Joel said tersely, "For starters, Alex Ben Raschid sits on the board of the bank that's considering my expansion loan. I'm strictly small potatoes, Sabrina. Sedikhan Petroleum could force me out of business in two months' time if they decided to exert a little muscle."

"There must be laws to prevent a company from doing that," Sabrina protested hotly. "Who is Alex Ben Raschid, some kind of dictator? I just can't believe you're giving in to him!"

"Do you think I like having them lean on me?" he asked harshly. "I'd like to tell them to go to hell, but this business means a lot to me. I've worked damn hard and invested every cent I could lay my hands on. There's no way I'm going to let it go down the drain. It may not be fair, but you're expendable, Sabrina," he finished bluntly.

The surge of rage that shook her prevented her from speaking for a moment. How dare Alex do this to her! The supreme arrogance of the action took her breath away. How vicious to take away a person's livelihood just to avenge a blow to his self-esteem. Somehow she hadn't believed him capable of such pettiness, and her disillusionment added fuel to her anger.

Mistaking her silence for despondency, Joel said with gruff sympathy, "I know you need the job, kid, and I'll give you a damn good reference." He began to toy with the pencil again, obviously wishing this interview were over. "Maybe if you can smooth over your differences with Ben Raschid we could work something out."

She leaped to her feet, her eyes blazing. "You expect me to go to him on my knees, begging for my job back?" she gritted, leaning forward and putting both hands on the desk. "I may be naïve, but I still believe that no one should give up his self-respect for money. I don't want to work for you any more, Joel." She drew a deep breath, trying to control herself. "I'm going to see Alex Ben Raschid all right but only to tell him what a grade-A bastard he is!"

She turned and stormed out of the office, past the startled receptionist, to the ancient red Volkswagen parked at the curb.

Five

The Sedikhan Petroleum Building was known to
everyone in Houston. A towering skyscraper, it
seemed to be composed entirely of reflecting glass
and was a miracle of modern architecture. When
it had officially opened a year before, the Sunday
Supplement had carried a four-page pictorial story
on it. Sabrina, however, didn't even notice the
much-touted exterior as she pulled into the parking lot. She walked determinedly into the lobby,
and after locating the executive offices in the
directory, entered the elevator and pushed the
button for the top floor. Ordinarily the plush lux-
ury of the building would have intimidated her,
but now the affluent surroundings only reminded
her of the arrogance of the man she was going
to see. That someone with such wealth could
be so ruthless, so callous, only added fuel to her
anger.

When the elevator door opened, she strode into
the lushly carpeted foyer like a young Amazon
going into battle. The outer office was occupied by
a sleek brunette at a mahogany desk. She looked
up with a dazzling smile that rapidly faded as she
took in the sight of Sabrina in her faded Levi's
and white oxford cloth shirt. "May I help you,
please?" she asked.

"I'd like to see Alex Ben Raschid. I'm Sabrina Courtney."

The brunette smiled tolerantly. "I'm afraid Mr. Ben Raschid is a very busy man. He never sees anyone without an appointment. Do you have an appointment?"

"I do not have an appointment, but I'm going to see Alex Ben Raschid *now*." The last word was said with such intensity that it caused even the confident receptionist to waver.

"I'll ring his private secretary, Miss Courtney," she said coolly, picking up the receiver, "but I don't think it will do any good. Mr. Ben Raschid never sees anyone unless they're expected."

"Oh, I'm expected," Sabrina said grimly. "I'll lay odds that Alex is expecting me."

The brunette looked puzzled as she spoke into the phone. She listened for a moment, her expression changing to one of shock, then she said briskly, "Right away, Miss Johnson," and replaced the telephone. "You're to go right in, Miss Courtney," she said to Sabrina. "Mr. Ben Raschid left orders that he would be available to you at any time."

"How kind of him," Sabrina said bitterly, only the surface meaning of the double entendre reaching the receptionist, to judge by the look on her face.

"It's the door on the left and straight to the end of the hall," she said, her glossy smile once more in place.

The door at the end of the hall opened to a luxurious office done in beige and orange, and the desk this time was occupied by a dark-haired woman in her middle thirties with an air of computerlike efficiency.

The secretary didn't even raise an eyebrow at Sabrina's appearance but said coolly, "I'm Velma

Johnson, Miss Courtney. I'm sorry you were kept waiting." She waved a perfectly manicured hand at a brown tweed couch. "Won't you sit down, and I'll order you some coffee. Mr. Ben Raschid is in conference with two department heads, but he should be through shortly.

Sabrina strode past her to the single door on the wall behind her desk. Turning the knob, she said emphatically, "Miss Johnson, I don't care if he's in conference with the King of Siam. I'm seeing him!"

The two older men seated in front of the large, teak executive desk looked up, startled at the intrusion. Sabrina ignored them as she walked across the wide expanse of plush, hunter green carpet, her whole attention fixed on the man behind the desk.

Alex Ben Raschid was dressed for business in a charcoal gray suit and vest, his white shirt contrasting sharply with his dark hair and golden tan. He was studying some papers in front of him as she walked in but looked up abruptly when one of the men broke off in the middle of a sentence. His ebony glance raked over her boldly, and a slow, mocking smile lit his face.

Velma Johnson, hurrying in behind her, broke in apologetically, "I'm sorry, Mr. Ben Raschid, I told her you were busy."

He rose to his feet in one lithe movement and came around the desk, "It's all right, Velma," he said coolly. "Sabrina is sometimes a little impatient, aren't you, darling?" He put an arm around her waist affectionately, but Sabrina could detect the steely strength beneath the casual embrace. "I suppose I should be flattered."

Flattered! "Alex, you are—"

"Yes, darling, I know," he interrupted smoothly. He turned to the two men. "If you'll excuse me, we'll continue this meeting at another time." As they began putting their papers into their briefcases, he turned to Velma Johnson. "See that I'm not disturbed until Miss Courtney leaves."

Sabrina caught a knowing exchange of glances between the two department heads and bit her lip in frustration. When the door finally closed behind them, she was positively seething. "I don't know what you think you accomplished by that little charade," she exploded, breaking away from Alex.

He seemed content to let her go, now that there was no longer an audience. He seated himself on the corner of the desk and crossed his arms, watching with all evidence of enjoyment the rage that illuminated her face. "I merely wanted to put a good façade on the situation," he drawled smoothly. "I wouldn't want you to be embarrassed the next time you meet the gentlemen."

"As I don't intend to see either man again, I don't see that your argument is valid," she said icily.

"You didn't like them?" he asked, raising a brow. "They're quite nice, but of course we'll avoid them if you've taken a dislike to them."

Sabrina mentally counted to ten before answering. "I don't even know them. But if they have anything to do with you, I wouldn't touch them with a ten-foot pole!"

"That's good, Sabrina, I wouldn't want any other man closer than that to you," he said softly.

"Will you stop talking inanities?" she asked furiously. "You know why I'm here. How could you do such an unspeakable thing? No, don't tell me. I'm sure it comes quite easily to such an insufferable egotist." She was pacing up and down the room as she spoke but stopped in front of him. "Did it ever occur to you here in your ivory tower that some people *need* to work for their living?"

There was a flicker of anger in the dark eyes that watched her, and a muscle jerked in his cheek. "I think when you get to know me better, Sabrina, you'll find I work quite hard. What's more, I provide jobs for thousands of employees."

"Is that what makes you think you can play God?" she asked scornfully, tossing her head.

He muttered a low oath. "Believe me, I'm leaning closer to Mephistopheles at the moment. You'd try the patience of a saint. Don't go too far, Sabrina." His tone was soft, but ominous. "You're no doubt ranting about the action I was forced into taking this morning."

"Forced?" she spat, her green eyes darkening to almost emerald with anger. "Who could have forced the great Alex Ben Raschid to get me fired?"

"Why, you did, Sabrina," he said mockingly. "If you'd agreed to come and live with me, none of this would have been necessary. If you'd come to the party yesterday, I would have offered you a job at Sedikhan Petroleum then."

"And just what would my duties have been?" she grated.

"Anything you like. Secretarial, sales, whatever suits you. I told you I'd let you set the pace"—he paused—"at least for a while." He stood up and moved slowly toward her and she backed away involuntarily. "The offer is still open, Sabrina," he said caressingly. "I wouldn't take away one job without providing another in its place—at double your present salary."

"And that's supposed to make it all right?" she asked incredulously." "How would you know I'd like your job? For your information, I was quite happy with the one I had. I don't want your darn, stuffy job!"

The flicker in his dark eyes leaped into flame as Alex's hands clamped on her upper arms. "You may enjoy flaunting that luscious body before strange men, but you'll have to give up your teasing little games. I find I'm curiously possessive of you, Sabrina." He pulled her closer so that the last words were muttered into her hair.

The magic of his sexual magnetism was pulling at her even as the words repelled. She could feel the erratic pounding of his heart and the heat of his body through his clothing. She reached up to push him away, but his hands slid down her arms to her wrists, pulling them behind her back and arching her body to fit his. His muscles were taut, his arousal shockingly obvious.

"See what you do to me?" he whispered huskily, his tongue exploring her ear. With little kisses he followed the line of her cheek until he reached her lips, and his mouth covered hers. He groaned, his tongue invading with an intimacy that caught at her breath. She made a sound between a moan and a sob. Too late she realized she should never have come here. His lovemaking was causing her to doubt even her reason for approaching him. Had it really been rage or had that been an excuse to once more come shivering to warm herself at this flame of physical pleasure?

He'd released her arms to pull her hips still closer to his in even greater intimacy. Free, she didn't push him away, instead she slipped her arms under his coat to press herself closer to him. He gave a husky laugh and swept her off her feet, then carried her to the massive executive chair behind the desk, where he cradled her on his knees possessively.

"Why do I feel this tenderness whenever I hold you in my arms?" he asked, his lips moving to caress the lobe of her ear. "Even when I'm wanting you so much I ache with it, I want to treat you as if you were Dresden china." His lips moved to the pulse point under her chin. "I knew you'd be angry that I'd pulled strings to get you fired, sweetheart, but I had to do it." His lips moved down to the hollow of her throat. "I couldn't take it. You can see that, can't you? Forgive me, Sabrina. I promise I'll make it up to you, love."

Perhaps it was those words, "Forgive me,"—so alien to Alex, she knew—but she was lost and felt only the need to give whatever he asked of her. Then he was kissing her again. His swift hands dispensed with the buttons of her shirt and the front fastening of her bra, freeing her breasts to his palms. She gasped as his fingers caressed and teased. When he looked down, a flush mottled his cheeks and his eyes glazed with desire. "Do you know, you have the most perfect breasts I've ever seen," he whispered. "They were meant to be loved." He lowered his lips to take one eager nipple in his mouth and she shuddered with the incredible sensation he evoked with his lips and tongue. Suddenly her hands were working at the buttons of his vest and shirt.

"Alex, accounting has finished—" Clancy Donahue broke off abruptly.

One moment she was cradled on Alex's lap, his lips at her breast, the next she was crushed to his chest, her head buried in his shoulder, his arms wrapped around her protectively.

"Damn you, Clancy," Alex's voice rumbled angrily beneath her ear. "I told Velma we weren't to be disturbed. What the hell do you mean breaking in here?"

"Damn! I'm sorry, Alex." Donahue's voice *definitely* sounded sorry. "Velma wasn't at her desk, and I knew you wanted this report." There was the sound of a hasty withdrawal and the closing of a door.

Alex's arms loosened their viselike hold as he put her a little away from him. "Now, where were we?" he murmured huskily.

But the moment of shock and embarrassment at Donahue's intrusion had flooded Sabrina with cold reason. She felt a sickness in the pit of her stomach at her own abysmal weakness. If Donahue hadn't come in, she would have yielded anything Alex demanded. She shook her head dazedly and pushed herself off his lap, her hands fumbling at the buttons of her shirt. Surprisingly, he let her go after one keen look at her face.

"I was afraid Clancy had blown it," he said, his lips curving in a wry smile as he watched her move away. She noted dully that he didn't bother to button the waistcoat her eager fingers had unfastened; perhaps he wanted to remind her of his power over her. It was quite an effective ploy, she thought miserably, shame darkening her face. There was no way she could deny she'd not only been submissive, but eager. How could she have been such a fool? Her shaking hands lifted to refasten the ponytail Alex had loosened, the movement pulling her shirt tight over her breasts. She looked up at the sound of his sharply indrawn breath.

"Don't be provocative, Sabrina. I'm within an inch of taking you right here and now. And we both know you wouldn't be unwilling very long, don't we?"

His question pierced her armor with fatal accuracy. Suddenly the tears that had been threatening rolled down her cheeks as she stared at him with the helplessness of a hurt fawn.

"Damn!" he swore softly. He was across the office and she was in his arms again. His embrace was almost sexless, a warm, protective enfolding only meant to comfort, not entice, as he held her for a long, peaceful moment. "Easy, sweetheart. Damn it, don't you know what that does to me? I think I'm back in cool control again and then you do something like that and it blows everything sky high." He drew a deep, shuddering breath. "I feel like I'm melting inside. God, I've never known anything like this in my life."

How many facets were there to his character, Sabrina wondered? He changed like a chameleon from one moment to the next. With a sigh she moved away from him. "I'm quite all right now," she said with fragile dignity.

His mouth twisted. "I wish I could say the same." He ran his fingers through his dark hair. "I don't usually find myself acting big brother to a woman I want to bed, nor do I generally seduce women in my office."

The faint note of accusation in his voice caused her to raise her chin in indignation. "I suppose that's my fault, too," she said. "I forced you to make love to me!"

"In a manner of speaking. You're a very desirable woman and your promiscuous behavior is an open invitation to any man."

"Promiscuous! How can you call my behavior promiscuous? I've done everything in my power to discourage you!"

His lips twisted cynically, and there was leaping anger in his dark eyes. "I appear to be excluded from your amorous propensities," he said harshly. "It's enough to give one an inferiority complex when you appear to be so overly generous with your favors with everyone else. Doesn't your lover object to your other men?"

"My lover?" Sabrina asked blankly.

"That young fool of a cowboy you kissed in front

of half of Houston," he said bitterly, "And who was the older man you were so intimate with in the box? Another lover?"

"Why not?" she said sarcastically, her voice rising. "If I'm a *femme fatale*, why not another man? Why not *ten* other men?"

He reached out and shook her. "Damn you, was that your lover?"

"Of course he's my lover," she said, almost hysterically. "They're all my lovers!"

"You bitch," he gritted, his hands tightening on her shoulders.

She felt a feverish excitement that ignored the danger inherent in taunting him. The pain and humiliation he'd inflicted on her were crying out to be revenged. "I told you I'd take as many lovers as I liked," she said wildly. "And there's nothing you can do about it."

Alex took a deep breath and suddenly the cool businessman was back, the dark eyes masked but emanating such power and menace that she would rather have faced the unleashed violence of the moment before. He released her very carefully and stepped back, buttoning his jacket and smoothing his hair casually. "I can do a great deal about it. I was prepared to be patient, but you've made me angry, Sabrina. I'm not waiting any longer. You'd better run along now," he said dismissingly, as he moved behind the desk. "I have an appointment in a few minutes."

She moved to the door dazedly, suddenly wishing she'd not lost her temper and taunted him. Alex Ben Raschid in this mood was a very dangerous man.

As she turned the knob of the door, he spoke behind her. "Oh, Sabrina," he said softly, almost absently, "beginning now, you're mine. I don't really care whether you acknowledge it or not, but if you let any other man so much as hold your hand, I promise you that you'll regret it."

The chill of steel sheathed in warm velvet . . . that's how his voice sounded, she realized, a shiver racing up her spine. She closed the door quietly behind her.

"How long are we going to stay here, Bree?" David asked hesitantly, a troubled frown creasing his forehead. He leaned against the trunk of a cottonwood tree and tipped his Stetson farther back on his head.

"Hold still, love," Sabrina commanded absently, her charcoal pencil moving rapidly across the sketch pad. "We've only been here for a little over a week." She glanced up with swift concern. "I thought you were having a wonderful time."

"I just think it's time for us to leave," David said haltingly.

Sabrina slowly closed the sketch pad and put it on the grass beside her. "Why, David?"

His sapphire gaze was fixed thoughtfully on the lacy pattern of the leaves above his head. "I just think it's time," he said huskily.

Something was definitely troubling him, and Sabrina had a good idea what it was. She'd been conscious of the strain since the moment they'd arrived. It would have been too much to hope that David wouldn't be even more aware than she. "Is it your father?" she probed gently.

"No." He smiled wistfully. "It's been fun being with Dad and working the ranch together like we did before." He was silent for a long moment. "It's Mother, Bree."

"She loves you very much, David."

"I know," he said. "I know she does. But I'm hurting her." His eyes fastened gravely on Sabrina's face. "Sometimes I can almost feel her pain and that hurts me, too. Why am I hurting her, Bree?"

"It's very complicated, love," Sabrina said throatily, looking away from him evasively. "Perhaps it only needs time to make it right."

"I don't think so," he said, biting his lip. "When she looks at me, it's as if she's searching for something and not finding it." His face clouded. "I try to be there for her, Bree, and sometimes for a moment or two I think I really am." He shrugged helplessly. "But then it slips away."

What could she say? She'd seen that expression on Sue's face and knew what David meant. How could she tell him it was the son who'd perhaps vanished forever his mother was searching for? His mother had been wrong in thinking she was ready to accept this stranger-child, and after a week Sabrina had doubts she would ever make the adjustment. It had been a mistake coming back to the ranch even for a visit.

"We'll only be staying a few more days," she said. She stood up and dusted off her jeans. "Will you be glad to get back to Gino and Angelina and all your flowers?"

He brightened immediately. "Yes." Then he frowned. "I hope Miranda's okay."

"Gino wouldn't let anything happen to any of your plants," Sabrina said comfortingly. She picked up her pencil and sketch pad. "Come on, lazybones. We've got to get back to the ranch. We're supposed to go to that party at Juan Mendoza's this evening."

David got obediently to his feet. "Do I have to go, Bree?" he sighed, as he trailed behind her to the tree where the horses were tied.

"Your parents don't ask much of us," Sabrina said. "Juan Mendoza is a very important man in the Cattleman's Association and the biggest rancher in the valley. I don't think Jess wants to offend him."

"Okay," David said absently, lifting his head to look at the rapidly darkening sky to the east. "It looks like we're going to get a real gullywasher."

"That's good isn't it, after that drought all last summer?"

He was still frowning uneasily at the rapidly building thunderheads. "Maybe," he answered. "Dad says the drought caused erosion along the river, and we've been getting an awful lot of rain lately. The river is almost over the banks now."

He gave her a leg up, then mounted himself and rode swiftly up the hill. Sabrina followed more slowly and paused for a moment on the rise. The wind swept through the cottonwoods. It stirred the tall grasses and caused an uneasy shiver in the mare she was riding. She patted the horse's neck, murmuring soothingly while she took in the sight of the lowering sky and a flash of lightning in the distance. Storms had always excited her, she felt a strange exhilaration that was close to the primitive.

With a kick she sent the mare racing after David's chestnut, tearing over the ground, passing David with a low laugh. "I'll see you at the house," she shouted, and the distance was covered in a matter of minutes. She reined in at the stable, competently unsaddled the mare, and put out feed and water. Then she ran up the porch steps and into the house.

Sue Bradford came hurrying into the hall from the general direction of the kitchen, a worried frown on her face. Tall, brown-haired and slim, she had always possessed a youthful vitality and cheerful enthusiasm. It was painfully disconcerting to see the expression of haunted sadness that had aged her so drastically in the past two years.

"I'm glad you're back," she said. "Jess just left for the south basin bordering the river. He wants David to join him as soon as possible. They're predicting a storm that will cause the river to crest and very likely flood the basin. The herd will have to be moved."

Sabrina turned at once toward the door. "David's probably at the stable by now. I'll go after him and we'll both ride out right away."

Sue was shaking her head. "Jess said to only send David. He has Pete Donaldson and Jake Montieth helping out. Thank God for neighbors you can count on in times like these." Her lips curved wryly. "Believe it or not, Jess wants you to go on to Mendoza's party. He's afraid of offending the great man if one of us doesn't attend."

"Jess wants me to go to a *party* when we may lose the south herd?" Sabrina asked incredulously.

Sue shrugged. "Don't ask me to fathom that man's thinking," she said dryly. "I've only had thirty-four years to work on it."

Sabrina shook her head. "It's crazy. Are you supposed to go the party and fiddle while Rome burns, too?"

Sue shook her head. "He knows better than to try to bulldoze me into leaving." Then she smiled comfortingly. "The situation isn't as bad as all that, Bree. Shifting the herd shouldn't take more than a few hours. I only want to be here to make sure they have dry clothes and hot food waiting when they straggle in like drowned rats."

"Then let me do that, Sue," Sabrina said stubbornly. "I don't even know Señor Mendoza very well."

The older woman reached out to shake her arm reprovingly. "Now stop arguing and do what you're told, Bree," she scolded with an affectionate grin. "You've got your assignment and I've got mine. All you have to do is make an appearance, present our apologies, and socialize for an hour or so. Now run along and get dressed while I go send David out to the basin." She turned and strode briskly out the screen door.

Sabrina grimaced ruefully as she mounted the stairs to the second floor. There was nothing she could do but accede to their requests, but she wasn't going to stay at Mendoza's party longer than absolutely necessary. It just might be the fastest duty appearance on record.

When she'd showered and washed her hair, she studied the clothes in her closet critically. She hadn't brought much with her, but there was one that might do, a sleeveless peach jersey sheath with a bateau neck that was deceptively modest in front but slashed to the waist in back. The warm peach shade showed off her tan and accented the flame of her loose, gleaming hair. She slipped into bone high-heeled sandals, and used a minimum of makeup—peach lip gloss, a touch of mascara, a brush of powder. Glancing casually into the full-length mirror, she decided that she would do. The Mendozas wouldn't be concerned with the appearance of such an unimportant guest anyway.

When she came downstairs, Sue was standing in the hall with an umbrella in her hand and a raincoat over her arm. "You're going to need these," she said briskly, and as if on cue there came a low rumble of thunder. "It's been pouring for the past fifteen minutes."

Sabrina slipped on the raincoat and belted it around her slim middle. "You're sure you want me to do this?"

"I'm sure," Sue said firmly, as she handed Sabrina the umbrella. "The keys are in the station wagon. You'd better not chance taking your

Volkswagen in weather like this. Tell Consuela Mendoza I'll call her tomorrow." Then she added with a frown, "Be careful crossing the river. The county supervisors have been going to replace that bridge with an elevated one for the past five years, but they've never gotten around to it."

Sabrina nodded. "Don't worry, I'll watch it." She hesitated, drawing a deep breath. "Sue, I've been meaning to tell you. David and I will be leaving soon. I have to find work and he shouldn't be away from Dr. Swanson for too long."

For a moment there was a flicker of unmistakable relief on Sue Bradford's face; seeing it, Sabrina's heart ached. Then it was gone and Sue was saying quietly, "Perhaps you're right. We'll talk about it later, Bree."

"Right." Sabrina turned away to keep Sue from seeing the suspicious mistiness in her eyes. "We'll talk about it later. I just thought you should know."

She ran to where the station wagon was parked, and in a few minutes she was driving through the storm. The wind whipped against the car in sheets; the windshield wipers were useless. Sabrina tensed with strain as she maneuvered the car almost blindly along the county road that crossed the Concho River.

As she approached the river the visibility improved and the rain slowed to just a steady downpour. It was only while she was actually crossing the bridge that Sabrina felt any real misgivings. The river was not yet out of its banks but it was dangerously close, and the engorged waters were already even with the floor of the bridge. Then she was across the span and was able to relax for the remaining ten-mile drive to the Mendoza ranch.

Her eyes widened as she drove into the flagstone courtyard and took in the fountain and the imposing bulk of the white stucco Spanish mansion. The gracious hacienda was as remote from the homey comfort of the Bradford ranch as it was possible to get.

At the front entrance the car door was opened immediately by a young, white-clad Mexican servant carrying a large black umbrella. Then she was shepherded into the brilliantly lit entrance alcove and the doors were ceremoniously opened by another smiling servant, who divested her of her rainwear and escorted her to her host.

Señor Mendoza shook Sabrina's hand warmly. "It is such a pleasure for my wife and me to welcome you to our home," he said cordially. A small, plump man, he was dressed faultlessly in a dark, tailored business suit and gray silk tie. He looked more like a Wall Street banker than a prosperous rancher, Sabrina thought. The woman beside him, equally cosmopolitan, was thin with high, elegant cheekbones and silver wings in her stylishly coiffed dark hair. Her black dress had the understated elegance of an original.

"Jess and Sue send their apologies, Señor Mendoza," Sabrina said politely. "They were unable to come due to an emergency at the ranch."

Mendoza nodded understandingly. "The storm, yes? I hope it's nothing serious."

She shook her head. "Merely a precaution. Jess felt the south-basin herd should be shifted. He and David are doing it now."

"A sound move," Mendoza agreed. "I'm desolate that my friend Jess was unable to be here, but we feel fortunate he was able to send such a lovely deputy."

Señora Mendoza's cool hand, held out in gracious greeting, didn't convey the same sense of welcome, Sabrina thought, though her murmured acknowledgment was cordial enough.

"Come let me introduce you to our other guests."

Señor Mendoza took Sabrina's arm and ushered her into a dimly lit lounge, elegantly decorated in various shades of blue.

There were perhaps fifty people clustered around the room. Soft music came over a stereo system, and a waiter with a tray of drinks circled unobtrusively. For the next fifteen minutes Mendoza acted the conscientious host, introducing her with scrupulous courtesy to his obviously affluent, elegantly dressed guests.

The center of the lounge had been cleared for dancing and Sabrina found no lack of partners as the evening progressed. She especially enjoyed the attentions of Jaime Mendoza, a dark, solemn young man in his early twenties, whom the Señor had introduced with some pride as his only son. Sabrina found Jaime as courteous and charming as his father, if a little lacking in humor, and rather boyishly entranced by her red hair. She was beginning to wonder if she'd stayed long enough to fulfill the duty Sue had imposed, when there was a sudden stir at the door. She glanced casually in that direction, but as there were several people blocking the way she couldn't determine the cause of the disturbance.

She turned her wandering attention back to Jaime, with whom she'd been dancing, but his attention had also been distracted. "My father's guest of honor has finally arrived," he announced. "His private jet was delayed by the storm."

"Really," Sabrina replied disinterestedly. The arrival of another of Señor Mendoza's business associates was hardly earthshaking.

But the new arrival seemed to hold a fascination for Jaime. "He is a very important man. My father was flattered when he requested advice on purchasing commercial property in this area."

Sabrina nodded politely. "I'm sure your father's advice would be invaluable to any businessman."

"That is true," Jaime agreed seriously. "He's considered quite shrewd."

Sabrina hid a smile. Ah-h, the self-importance of the young.

"Pardon me, Señor Mendoza, I believe your father would like to speak to you." The low drawl stopped her breath and froze her blood. She stopped dancing so suddenly that Jaime looked down at her in surprise.

He turned to the man standing beside them. "Mr. Ben Raschid!" he exclaimed, smiling ingratiatingly, though obviously at a loss as to why so illustrious a guest would deliver a message ordinarily sent by a servant.

Alex Ben Raschid nodded in acknowledgment, and with one smooth movement pulled Sabrina out of the young man's arms and into his own. "You wouldn't want to leave the lady alone in the middle of the dance floor," he said, smiling wickedly. Jaime stood looking at them for a moment, only daring the slightest expression of suspicion to touch his features before turning and going in search of his father.

Alex propelled Sabrina's stiff body around the dance floor. The low voices of the other guests, the clink of glasses, the music, all seemed to exist outside her frame of reference. Her body moved mechanically in time with his; her mind was numb.

As if angry at her lack of response, Alex's arms tightened around her waist and she was pulled so close to him she could feel every line of his taut, masculine body as they moved to the music. His face was buried in her hair and she could feel his warm breath in her ear. "You've caused me a great deal of trouble, you know," he murmured, his hand rubbing sensuous circles in the small of her back.

She drew a deep, shuddering breath. "I assume this is not a coincidence."

"Hardly," he said, sounding quite amused.

"How did you know where to find me?" She threw back her head to look into his face.

"You were in the Mendoza box at the rodeo. I discovered from your friend Angelina that you and your lover had left town. She refused to tell me any more than that. The rest was a matter of probing and maneuvering."

"At which, I haven't a doubt, you're a past master."

"Yes," he said coolly, "I am."

"Then your investigation—excuse me, your 'probing,' as you put it—must have brought to light the fact that Jess Bradford isn't one of my lovers! I'm sorry to prove your assessment of my character wrong in this case. I'm sure it must have been a big disappointment to you."

"Jess Bradford may not be on your list," he growled, "but his son is evidently retaining his place in your affections." His hand tightened on her waist. "Are you still sleeping with him?"

"You bastard," Sabrina said deliberately. "I'm here because I want to be here, and it's no business of yours what I do." Her lips twisted. "Though I must admit you made it easier to come to a decision. I suddenly found I had a good deal of free time on my hands, thanks to your intervention."

"You know I would have given you a job," he said roughly. "You didn't have to run away with that damned cowboy." His dark eyes narrowed as he took in the angry emerald of her eyes, the defiant tilt of her chin. "But you weren't running away *with* him, were you, Sabrina?" he asked slowly. "You were running away *from* me. I frightened you in the office that day."

"No!" she snapped. He must never know that the real source of her fear of him was the power he held over her emotions. He had weapons enough in the battle being waged between them. She would not provide him with additional ammunition.

"I think 'yes,' " he said consideringly, his gaze raking her face, weighing the quivering lips and the uncertainty that lay behind the defiance in her eyes. "I meant to frighten you," he said. "Not enough to make you run away, just enough to keep you out of anyone else's bed until I'd gotten you into mine. You reacted a bit more strongly than I'd gauged."

"Why should I be frightened of you?" she asked shakily, her brave façade crumbling under the driving force of his personality. "I'm my own person. I have my own thoughts and my own goals. I run my life to suit myself, Alex Ben Raschid."

He smiled at her and she caught her breath. There was no mockery in the smile. It was as if, perceiving the victory to be his, he'd discarded all antagonism. It was a tender smile, enfolding her in its glowing warmth. Her eyes widened with surprise as they met his, and something passed between them that was at once as strong as an electric current and as delicate as a gossamer thread. Neither desire nor anger, that ephemeral touching, it was a rapport she could see was as disturbing to Alex as it was to her.

He pushed her head down against his shoulder and they moved silently to the music. She closed her eyes helplessly against the tide of heat that seemed to fill her every limb with a languor and sweetness that was unbelievably right. His hand was buried in her hair and he stroked it sensuously.

"Do you know why you should be afraid of me?" he asked huskily. "I'll tell you. I want you so much that I want to absorb you into myself. I want to be so close to you that there's no Sabrina Courtney any more, just an extension of Alex Ben Raschid. I want your thoughts, your emotions, and your body." She felt a shudder run through him. "Oh, yes, I want that body of yours," he said raggedly. "I haven't been able to think of anything else for the last two weeks. I keep seeing your hair spread out on that damn blanket and feeling your body move under mine." He felt the quiver that ran through her at his evocative words, and his lips brushed the silken skin at her temple, savoring the pulsebeat with the tip of his tongue. "I hate you for what you're doing to me. I can't get the scent and feel of you out of my mind. Would you like to know how many women I've taken to bed since you ran away?"

She would have pulled away from him, but he defeated her with merciless strength. "No, damn you, don't stiffen up on me. It's you I wanted, not them. A few of them were quite accomplished," he said roughly, "and God knows I wanted to get you out of my system. I thought they would erase this crazy hunger I have for you, but they didn't. After I'd finished with them, I still wanted you just as much. More. And toward the end it made me sick to touch them. I was like a damn eunuch."

The pain that his word evoked was incredible in its intensity. The thought of Alex in bed with another woman, making love to her, enjoying her accomplished caresses, their bodies wrapped together in a passionate embrace. Alex making another woman feel this dark magic that made her a helpless captive in his arms.

"Please. Let me go," she begged, trying to twist away, her eyes tormented. She felt if she stayed in his arms one more second she'd die of the agony he'd inflicted with such callous disregard.

"You haven't been listening, Sabrina," he said grimly. "Do you think I've told you all this to hurt you? We may both be damned before it's over, but I *can't* let you go!"

"Hurt me? You could never hurt me!" she denied wildly. "You have to care about someone to be hurt by them. You mean nothing to me, Alex Ben Raschid. You could have a hundred women and I wouldn't care!"

With a desperate wrench she broke away, and ignoring the curious stares of the other dancers stalked blindly from the room. She wanted only to get away from him, from the words that had torn the protective bandage from emotions now throbbing and raw as new wounds.

She ran down the hall, opened a door, and slipped inside. There were no lights on; she could only see the vague outlines of table and chairs in a formal dining room. She leaned against the closed door, welcoming the anonymity of the darkness as would an animal in pain. Her breath came in little, sobbing gasps as she let the realization roll over her. Oh God, she loved him!

She felt sick. She'd gone through so many emotions in the last few minutes she felt as though she were in shock. How had it happened? She'd fought so hard not to care for him. She'd told herself it was only physical, that he'd merely caught her imagination as any attractive man might have done. She'd tried to erase the memory of the tenderness that had surged through her that afternoon on the beach when he'd revealed his background. How she'd shuddered at the treatment of him by his parents! How soft and weak she'd gone when she'd glimpsed the great vulnerability hidden behind that tough façade. She'd tried to ignore those flashes of wry humor that appeared so unexpectedly. And she'd been scrupulously careful not to think about those rare moments when he'd enfolded her in that gentle, protective cloak of affection. She'd blocked it out, ignored it, rejected it with everything that was in her, but at the thought of him with another woman the truth had struck her with the force of a blow. She'd felt as angry and betrayed as if they'd been married a dozen years.

Her lips twisted bitterly in the darkness, the tears ran helplessly down her cheeks. Marriage? Permanence would have no place in Alex Ben Raschid's scheme of things. He wanted her now, but how long would it be after he possessed her before his passion faded and he went back to those other women he'd spoken of so callously? He'd never mentioned love, only raging hunger, possessiveness, blind and overwhelming desire. He admitted to obsession, but not love.

Lord, how stupid could she get? As if she didn't have enough problems in her life she had to fall in love with a man as dominant and demanding as Alex. Even if she accepted the little he had to give her, he would claim every particle of her emotional and physical response for the time they would be together. How could she possibly grant him that when there was David to think about?

She wiped her eyes childishly with the back of her hand. It was too late to stop herself from loving Alex, but she must find some way to keep him from twisting her life so she'd never be able to straighten it out again.

She shivered as she remembered how difficult it had been to resist his sexual expertise when she'd thought what she was feeling was only physical attraction. How much harder it would be now that she'd admitted to herself he could be the most important part of her life. One thing was certain, Alex's mere physical presence would quell any resistance she could make. For she would be fighting not only him, but herself. Her love for him would be as formidable an ally as he could wish, for she wanted desperately to belong to him in all ways.

She reached a shaking hand to her temple, which was beginning to ache fiercely. She was so broken and confused that she couldn't seem to think straight. She certainly couldn't risk seeing Alex until she could defend herself against him. She would have to leave at once before she saw him again.

As she reentered the living room, she was immediately approached by Señor Mendoza. "Sabrina," he said, "I have been looking for you."

Her smile was strained as she said, "I wasn't feeling very well and I wanted to get some air. I thought it might help my head, but I'm afraid it hasn't. I'll have to go home."

The sympathy in Mendoza's dark eyes deepened as he took in the paleness of her cheeks. "It's true, you don't look well at all," he said, "but you're not to go home tonight. That is why we were searching for you. Jess called and said he was worried about the bridge supports. He would prefer that you not try to cross the bridge in the dark tonight. I naturally told him we would be happy to have you as our guest. My wife will show you to a guest room."

"I'm staying here tonight?" she repeated dazedly.

"It will be our pleasure," he assured her. "But why don't you sit down. I will get you a drink." He disappeared into the crowd.

She stood there, frozen, her eyes automatically searching the guests until she spied the figure she was looking for. Alex stood in a corner, unaware of her, absently looking down at his drink, while the man talking to him was eagerly explaining something to him. Her gaze went lovingly over the tall, virile strength of him while a tenderness filled her that was frightening in its intensity. Stay in the same house with Alex tonight? The intimacy of the mere idea was wildly appealing.

Suddenly he looked up and their eyes met across the room. Her breath caught in her throat. He put down his drink on a nearby table, left the man he was talking to as if the poor fellow didn't exist. The moment she realized he was coming toward her, she became panic stricken. She couldn't face him. Not now. She turned and ran from the room, down the hall, and out the front door.

Six

The rain was falling steadily, and the young servant was still on duty outside with his big, black umbrella. She brushed him aside and ran out to the far end of the courtyard where the station wagon was parked. She was wet through in seconds but she didn't even feel the cold. Her only thought was flight. She jumped into the driver's seat, turned on the ignition, and in a moment she was driving out of the courtyard and onto the access road as the boy in the vestibule stared bewilderedly after her.

The panic goading her gradually abated as she continued to drive. This had been a crazy thing to do, driving off into the night like some soap-opera heroine. Driving the car made her feel more in control, though, and slowly the ability to think logically returned. Where was she going? She couldn't drive around in the rain all night. She certainly couldn't return to the Mendoza house. She'd left her purse and belongings when she'd panicked, so she couldn't drive into town and stay at a hotel. There was only one course of action: to try the bridge. She'd drive to the approach and stop and take a look at it. If it appeared safe, she'd go for it. If not, she'd have to resign herself to parking somewhere along the road and spending the night in the station wagon.

The pounding of the pain in her head seemed to keep tempo with the rain on the roof. As she drove the rain dwindled to a fine drizzle, and now that visibility was improved her foot pressed harder and harder on the accelerator; the car flew along the country road. The back of her neck was rigid with tension as she crested the last hill and started down the other side, her eyes straining to make out the dim outlines of the bridge in the darkness.

She didn't notice the water until the station wagon's wheels hit it with such violence that muddy water sprayed in all directions, completely obscuring the windshield! For one terrible moment she thought she might overshoot and drive straight into the icy waters of the river. But the engine cut off abruptly, and she hurriedly rolled down the glass and stuck her head out the window. She was surrounded by water almost up to the car door handles.

The Concho had obviously overflowed the basin at the bottom of the hill, and her car had landed right in the middle of the flooded road. She leaned her head on the steering wheel in sheer frustration. She was stuck, she realized dismally. There was no possibility of backing the station wagon out. The engine was no doubt thoroughly flooded.

She could see the muddy, yellow water begin to trickle in a thin stream under the door; it would be only a matter of minutes before the interior of the car was flooded.

She gave a resigned sigh as she realized there was only one thing to do. She'd have to abandon the car and climb back up the hill on foot. Once she reached the upper slopes, she'd be safe from the rising water, and only have to worry about finding shelter or stopping a passing motorist.

Neither prospect was very promising, she thought gloomily. She was miles from the nearest inhabited ranch house and this particular road led only to the bridge and the few ranches beyond.

She slipped off her flimsy high heels and threw them on the back seat. She rolled down the window as far as it would go, then wriggled feet first through the narrow opening. She gave a little gasp as she immediately sank into the cold, muddy water which swirled around her waist. She took a few tentative steps away from the car; it was hard going. Mud sucked at her stocking feet. She slogged ahead with determination, spurred on by thoughts of the poisonous water moccasins inhabiting the river banks, and she was out of the water and mounting the lower reaches of the hill in double-quick time. Chilled and reeling from the ordeal, she could at least be grateful that the falling rain was washing away the filthy scum of the river water.

As she approached the top of the hill, she suddenly saw the beam of headlights coming fast up the other side. Without thinking of anything but preventing the driver from coming to the same fate she had, she ran to the middle of the road, waving her arms urgently. "Stop! You've got to stop."

As the car crested the hill, she realized it was traveling too fast to halt before it reached her. She stood paralyzed in the beam of the oncoming headlights knowing the car would hit her but unable to move.

The driver also must have realized the hopelessness of attempting to stop because he turned the wheel violently to the right. Miraculously only the left fender brushed her, throwing her to the ground. The car plowed into the shallow ditch at the side of the road. She struggled to her feet, racing to the wrecked car and whimpering over and over to herself, "Oh please let him be all right. Please, don't let him be hurt." Then with a surge of relief she realized the driver's door was opening. "Oh, thank God," she gasped, as she reached the car.

"You'd do well to pray. I'm on the verge of murdering you, Sabrina," Alex said grimly, getting out. His face was pale with emotion and there was a small cut at his hairline that was bleeding profusely.

She wasn't even surprised. It seemed a logical extension of this nightmare evening for this to be Alex. "I thought I'd killed you," she said numbly, conscious of a sudden weakness in her knees.

"You damn near did, and yourself, too, you crazy woman," he snapped. "What kind of trick did you think you were pulling, standing in the middle of the road trying to flag someone down on a night like this?" He grabbed her shoulders. "I almost killed *you!*"

She collapsed against him, sobbing, burrowing against him as if he were the only security she would ever know. He stood still, holding her softness to him securely, but she could tell by the unyielding tightness of his hard, muscular body that he was still shaken and angry.

"It was the flooding," she gasped between sobs. "The valley is flooded at the bottom of the hill. I was trying to warn you."

"So you almost killed us both," he said dryly. "Not the brightest solution."

"I'm sorry," she whispered miserably, burrowing closer to his warmth. "You're right. It was a stupid thing to do."

He was perfectly still for a long moment and when he spoke there was a note of surprise in his voice. "You must be in worse shape than I thought," he said. "I've never heard you so docile. Let me take a look at you." He pushed her away and surveyed her critically for a moment, taking in the bare feet, the sodden clothes clinging to her shivering body, her hair plastered to her head and hanging in lank strands about her pale face. He swore softly and fluently as he took off his suit jacket and wrapped it around her. "You little fool, you're half drowned."

The jacket was warm from his body and she hugged it to herself gratefully. Then she noticed guiltily that the rain was wetting him almost as thoroughly as it had her and he was hurt and bleeding as well. She started to take off the jacket and hand it back to him.

"Keep it on," he ordered. "You'll be damn lucky if you don't get pneumonia as it is." He knelt and peered under the car for a moment, then straightened and said disgustedly, "The back axle is broken. I thought I heard it give when I hit the ditch."

"You can't drive it?" she asked.

"Not likely," he said, grimacing. "And we certainly can't stay here. We need warmth and shelter." He reached into the car, turned off the lights, and then slammed the door. "This is your territory, is there a ranch or a cabin nearby?"

Sabrina shook her head. "The Mendoza Ranch is closest and that's almost ten miles, and the Bradford spread is across the bridge."

"A barn? A cave? Think!"

"There's a vacant ranch house about a half mile from here," she said slowly. "The Circle C."

"Which way?" he asked.

She pointed wordlessly, and he took her arm and set off briskly, half carrying her along. By the time they'd reached the turnoff to the ranch, she was breathless but the exercise had warmed her considerably.

"Not very imposing," Alex commented, as they reached the front porch of the cedar ranch house, which was at the top of a rise overlooking the highway. "But at least we'll be dry. We'll have to break in if we can't find an open window."

"That won't be necessary," Sabrina said calmly. She reached under the window sill of the left front window, withdrew a magnetic key box, and extracted the front door key. She opened the door and turned to meet his questioning stare. "I used to live here," she said simply. "When my parents died, Jess Bradford bought the property, but he had no use for the house itself. It's been deserted for a number of years."

"You're full of surprises," Alex said, following her into the hall.

The dark house looked terribly desolate, Sabrina thought sadly, looking around. All the furnishings and mementos that had made the place dear to her were stored under covers in the Bradfords' barn. Only unwanted pieces too dilapidated to be of any real use were left—a couch in the living room, a broken chair in the kitchen. The old drapes had also been left at the windows, as they hadn't fit the windows of the apartment in Houston. Everything was covered with a thick layer of dust.

Alex fumbled in his pocket for his lighter. The small flame helped him appraise their surroundings. He disappeared into the room to the left of the hall. "There's a fireplace in here," he called briskly. "If we can make a fire, we can at least dry off." He was taking charge again as he always would, his vitality bringing the dead house back to life.

"There should be some wood in the wood box in the cellar," Sabrina offered quietly, watching as he strode from room to room, reconnoitering the situation for assets and liabilities so he could grasp and control it.

"You supply our every need," he said lightly. "I don't suppose there is anything you could change into upstairs?" She shook her head silently. "Too bad," he said, and striding to the living room he ripped the drapes from the window and tossed them to her. "Get out of those wet clothes. All of them," he ordered. "I'll get that wood and start a fire."

She stared at the cream and chocolate-striped drapes in her hand and smiled, recalling a similar scene from *Gone With the Wind.* Well, she wasn't Scarlett O'Hara, she thought wryly, and she didn't even have a needle and thread, so there would be no fabulous gown created from these drapes!

She shed her wet clothes hurriedly and, wrapping one of the panels around her body sarong-like, belted it at the waist with one of the ties. She wrinkled her nose in distaste at the musty smell as she tossed the other panel around her shoulders like a shawl.

Alex entered the room carrying a load of wood, and without a glance at her deposited it near the fireplace and set about building a fire. Soon it was blazing brightly and he took the time then to wipe the wound on his forehead. Now that it was no longer bleeding, it appeared to be only a small cut, she noticed with relief.

He looked her over and his mouth went up at the corners. "Very fetching."

"Well, you're no Rhett Butler either," she said crossly, knowing she looked a sight.

He grinned at the reference. "Well, frankly, my dear, I don't give a damn," he mimicked in a fair Gable imitation.

She chuckled.

"Come over here," he commanded, putting some additional kindling on the blaze. She obediently crossed to him and stood with her hands out, basking in the warmth of the fire.

"Not too close," he warned. "There's no screen." He rose lithely and, crossing to the dilapidated, dark brown couch against the wall, he stripped it of the four large seat cushions and tossed them in front of the fireplace.

"Your hair is still wet," he said, frowning accusingly as she settled down in front of the blaze.

"It will dry," she said contentedly, soaking up the heat from the fire like a contented kitten.

He stood up and left the room, coming back with two pieces of cloth that she recognized as the kitchen curtains. She chuckled. "What would you have done if we'd taken all the curtains with us?"

"I'd have managed," he said confidently, and she knew it was true. He would always manage to wrest whatever he wanted from the world. He was that kind of man. He knelt beside her. "Bend over."

She obeyed and he briskly toweled her hair, not stopping until it was almost dry. Sitting a little away from her on the cushion, he started to dry his own hair. "You grew up here?" he asked, his dark gaze on her face.

She nodded, staring into the fire dreamily. "I was born and raised in this house," she said softly. "Then, when my parents died, I moved in with the Bradfords and later to Houston when I went away to college. But I always wanted to come back. I'm not really a city girl."

"You seem to have acclimated remarkably well."

She knew he was referring to her supposed affair with David, but decided to ignore it. As if he, too, were reluctant to enter a discordant note in the harmony of the moment, Alex went on to other subjects. They talked for a long time, with an amazingly easy intimacy, and when a silence finally did lapse, it was deliciously comfortable.

"Why have you fought me, Sabrina?" he asked suddenly. "I can give you almost anything in the world. What do you want?"

She looked at him, his dark, tousled hair, the white shirt open to the waist revealing the strong, corded muscles and the springy pelt of virile, dark hair on his chest. You. Only you, she thought.

She drew her knees up and rested her chin on them, gazing dreamily into the fire. "I guess I want what my parents had," she said softly. "I want to build a good life. I want roots and an affection that will only get stronger as the years pass."

"Your parents must have been unusual people," he said quietly.

"No, they were really very ordinary people. They just loved each other," she said huskily.

They were both lost in their own thoughts and there was a long silence in the room. The only sound was the crackle of the burning logs and the light rhythm of their breathing.

"Sabrina?"

Her eyes flew to his, startled out of her meditation. And what she saw there caused her to draw a sharp, shallow breath.

"You know you're going to belong to me tonight," he stated simply.

She had known for some time, she thought calmly. There was only one fitting conclusion to this intimacy of their time together. "Yes," she whispered, lost in the darkness of his eyes. "I know that, Alex."

"Come here," he said, holding out his hand, and she obeyed him wordlessly. She knelt facing him, not touching him, just looking into his eyes and waiting. Her hair was a wild, flaming areole around her face, her eyes deep emerald in the flickering light, and her lips parted in unknowing anticipation. His gaze lingered over every feature like a caress.

He reached out slowly and pushed the improvised shawl away from her shoulders. His eyes fixed with intent absorption on the satin of her shoulders as his hands closed on them almost gingerly and he brought her carefully, surely into his arms.

"Alex," she said huskily, her eyes suddenly shadowed with doubt. "It's not just because of that passion you mentioned you had for redheads, is it? You don't have to pretend you care for me, but I'd like to know I mean more to you than that." Her lips were trembling as she tried to smile. "I always have hated to be just one of a crowd."

One large hand reached out slowly to wrap itself in her long, silky tresses. "God, no, love," he said thickly. "I've never felt anything like this before in my life." His eyes were ebony stains in the bronze tautness of his face and his expression was oddly grave. "I've been thinking quite a bit lately about those redheads in my past. I remember reading a poem once about 'the mystic memory of things to come.'" His hand was combing gently through her hair in a deliciously soothing motion. "I've had a crazy notion since I met you that maybe there is such a thing. Perhaps I was searching for my own sweet redhead among that faceless throng." A tender smile curved his lips. "You certainly took your time about appearing on the scene, sweetheart. I'd almost given up."

Sabrina felt her throat tighten achingly and for a moment she didn't think she could speak. She'd expected a mocking reassurance, not this moving gift he'd given her with such simple eloquence.

"That sounds remarkably romantic for a man who believes love is a word for children," she said shakily.

"It's all your fault," he said, tilting her head to look into her eyes. "I never wanted to feel like this about any woman. Since the moment I saw you, I've been trying to convince myself that it was just lust I felt for you." He touched the softness of her lips with a finger so gentle that she had a fleeting memory of David and his golden Miranda. "God knows, I feel enough of that, but there's more, too. I want to *cherish* you." He shook his head helplessly. "Lord, that's an old-fashioned word, but it's the only one that fits. I want to care for you. I want to wrap you in all the gauze of tenderness and all the velvet of gentleness that still exists in this harsh world of ours. I can't bear to think of you in pain or need." He took a deep breath. "Will you let me cherish you, Sabrina?"

"Oh, yes," she said huskily, feeling a surge of love and delight that made her dizzy. "I want that, Alex."

He slowly pushed her down on the cushions and his hands were shaking a little as he undid the tie at her waist and carefully opened the cream and brown folds, spreading them on the cushion like silken butterfly wings. He groaned as he stared down at the graceful curves and shadows revealed to him in the flickering firelight. "You're all flame and snow and a sweet, burning grace."

Unable to wait any longer, he left her for a moment to rapidly strip off the rest of his own clothing and rejoined her, pressing her deep into the cushions, their bodies flesh to flesh so that she could feel his bold arousal. How much more graceful and beautiful was his hard muscular beauty than her own soft curves, she thought dreamily. She hadn't realized until now that broad, supple shoulders tapered to a slim middle and tight, muscular buttocks could have this almost singing symmetry.

He slowly lowered his lips with a deliberateness that caused her to hold her breath in anticipation. Then his warm tongue flicked out to caress one taut nipple and she stiffened with unbearable tension. She could feel her breasts swell and harden beneath that teasing tongue as if on command. Alex's hands closed around the fullness of those burgeoning mounds, weighing them in his palms, while his lips suckled lightly at the sensitive nipples. She made a little whimpering sound deep in her throat and he glanced up with a flicker of satisfaction. "That's right, darling," he said hoarsely. "Burn for me. Tell me how much you want me."

But she couldn't tell him. It was all too much. She could only make those little cries of desire and entreaty as his teeth pulled gently at the taut, pink rosette while his hands began a rhythmic kneading motion that was incredibly erotic. Her hands reached out blindly, running over the smooth, brawny copper of his shoulders to encircle his neck and pull him closer to her breasts.

She felt him shudder against her. "Touch me," he ordered raggedly. "I love to feel your hands on me. Do you know how often I've lain in bed and thought about your hands caressing me, loving me." His own hand reached up to take one of her hands from his shoulder. He brought it to his lips, his tongue stroking her palm. She shivered, her breath catching in her throat. She hadn't known that soft, vulnerable hollow could possibly generate this tingling awareness in every nerve in her body. Then, his dark eyes gazing compulsively into hers, he carried her hand to that taut hardness of his belly, holding it firmly against his warmth. "Touch me," he urged again.

She wanted to touch him. The hard flesh of his stomach had an almost magnetic attraction for her. The light springy dusting of hair beneath her palm felt delightfully abrasive as her hand moved over him curiously. His body was so different from her own, she thought absently. So hard where she was soft, so rough where she was smooth, so aggressive where she was pliant. Almost without thinking her hand curled about that warm aggression, holding him with loving tenderness.

She dimly heard Alex inhale sharply and his body bucked convulsively. She glanced up swiftly in concern. "Did I hurt you?" she asked.

"Oh, I'm hurting all right," he gasped, his lips curving wryly. "But for heaven's sake don't stop!"

Her hand tightened around him and he bucked again, his eyes closing while a shudder went through every muscle of his body. "Maybe you'd better stop after all," he said hoarsely. "I can't take much more of this." He opened his eyes and they were glazed and intent. "And I want to touch you, too, love." He reached down and gently removed her hand from him. "Lord, I feel cold and lonely without you," he whispered, taking a deep breath. "I can't wait to have your sweet warmth chaining me to you." He swiftly parted her legs and slipped a hand between them, the tips of his fingers moving in light, rhythmic patterns on the inside of her thighs, until she could feel the center of her being tighten and convulse in tempo with that tantalizing touch. She was writhing beneath his manipulations, her breath coming in little gasps, and she instinctively tried to close her thighs to capture and hold those maddening hands that were giving her only enough to drive her out of her mind.

"No, little flame," he said softly, looking up at her face, his own expression beautifully sensual. "Don't close me out." His fingers moved intricately and she suddenly cried out, her body arching in that age-old offering of woman, as an incredible sensation shot through her. "God, you're responsive." His hand moved again. "And so fantastically tight. I can't wait even a moment more for you. Are you ready for me, love?"

Was she ready for him? She felt as if she were going up like a skyrocket with every word he was speaking, with every motion of those magical, tormenting fingers.

He didn't wait for an answer, but gently widened the opening of her thighs and leaned forward to kiss her lingeringly on the mouth, his tongue entering to explore the moist interior with a hunger that took her breath, and caused her own tongue to seek his with an equal urgency.

Then he was surging forward and her cry of surprise and pain was smothered against his lips. He lifted his head, his expression dazed. "So tight," he murmured. His eyes widened incredulously. "My God . . ." he breathed, his gaze flying to her face.

Why was he waiting, she wondered wildly. The pain had only lasted for an instant and now this feeling of being beautifully, fantastically full of him was absolutely mind-blowing. But as much as she had of him, she wanted more.

"Alex, please," she gasped. "I *need* you."

There was an expression of almost pained pleasure on his face. "Dear Lord, and I need you," he choked. "I'm burning up, sweetheart." Then he was moving, in a driving rhythm that succeeded in satisfying that need while creating a feverishly molten new one.

She had the sensation that she was falling off

the edge of the world into a dazzling place of sheer, tactile pleasure. His hot words breathed in her ear were almost as arousing as his driving body, urging her to move with him, telling her how much her breasts pleased him, how exciting he found the way she clung to him.

Then the tension was mounting toward the final explosion of sensation, and she instinctively arched to meet each forceful thrust with an eagerness that caused Alex to close his eyes in an agony of pleasure. How beautiful he was with that expression of blind sensuality on his face, she thought dazedly. It filled her with an almost primitive satisfaction that it was the enjoyment of *her* body that brought him this exquisite torment. That every movement of her hips, every touch of her hands could cause this strong man to gasp and shudder with the need that was tearing them both apart.

Her legs tightened around him, her hands curving around his hips to cup the hard, sculptured line of his buttocks in her palms. He felt so *good*. Then she was pulling him toward her, matching his rhythm with one of her own.

Alex's eyes flicked open and he was gazing down at her, his dark eyes glazed. "God, little flame," he gasped, the bronze muscles of his chest heaving with the force of his breathing. She could see the pulse in his throat racing like a triphammer. "It's too good. It can't be real."

But it was real, gloriously, excitingly real. And when the tension snapped and they were tossed headlong into the final storm of feeling that was like no other, that was real, too. There was nothing less dreamlike on the face of the earth than the man above her who cried out in hoarse, almost guttural satisfaction, and clutched her to him while the whole world exploded around her and left her clinging to him like a child in the darkness.

She was vaguely conscious, in that moment of dazed euphoria, of Alex shifting positions to lie beside her on the cushions, enfolding her in the shelter of his arms and pushing her head into the hollow of his shoulder. She could feel the thunder of his heart beneath her ear and the light dew of perspiration on the dark golden skin that was her pillow. Her tongue darted out in lazy curiosity to taste the brawny smoothness of his shoulder. It was warm and slightly salty, and somehow deliciously exciting even in this moment of complete repletion.

Evidently Alex also found it exciting, for the thunder accelerated beneath her ear and he drew a deep breath that was more of a shudder. "God, don't do that, love," he gasped, his arms tightening around her. "Give me a couple of minutes to recover before you try any experiments that might lead down that particular road."

"I was just curious," Sabrina said dreamily, nestling her head back and forth on his shoulder like a kitten on a favorite satin cushion. "I wanted to know how you taste."

She could feel his chuckle reverberating beneath her ear, and his hand was gently stroking the silky hair at her temple. "And did you enjoy it, little flame?"

"Oh yes, very much," she said softly. Then she lifted her head to look into his face with bright, curious eyes. "Do you taste like that all over?"

He stared at her for a moment in blank surprise and then started to laugh, shaking his head in rueful amusement. "I haven't the slightest idea, but I'd be delighted for you to find out for yourself." He held up a hand. "In a few minutes, that is."

Sabrina frowned. "Am I being too aggressive,

Alex?" she asked uncertainly, her green eyes darkening to a troubled emerald as she gazed down at him.

"Lord no, sweetheart," Alex said huskily, his hand combing through the silky length of her hair with an almost sensual pleasure. "It's just that you're such a surprise to me that you've caught me off guard. I've never had the experience of wanting a woman again almost the instant I've left her. It's shaken me up a little." He pulled her lips down to meet his own in a long, soft kiss of dizzying sweetness. "There's not a thing in the world wrong with you, little flame," he said thickly when their lips parted. "There couldn't be anything more perfect than what we've just had together."

"I didn't think so," she said lightly, trying to hide how his words had moved her. "But it's always nice to have one's opinion confirmed by a man of your experience."

"Experience," Alex repeated slowly, his body stiffening against her own. His expression darkened grimly as he gazed up into her bewildered face. "I'd forgotten about that." With a swift movement he shifted her aside and was rolling off the cushions away from her. He snatched up the silky drapery he'd removed so eagerly such a short time before and tossed it to her. "Cover up," he said tersely. "We have some talking to do."

"Talking?" Sabrina asked warily.

She gazed down at the cream silk on her lap for a moment before she slowly shook out the folds and wrapped the length around her like a cloak. His words as well as his sudden rejection had shocked her out of the dazzling physical euphoria she'd been feeling only seconds before. She lifted a shaking hand to brush a lock of hair away from her face and moistened her lips nervously. She supposed she should be grateful that Alex had brought the real world back into focus for her, but instead she felt only an aching sense of loss.

Her gaze ran lingeringly over him as he sat naked in the firelight, a discreet distance from her own position on the cushion. He'd made no effort to veil his own nudity, she noticed with a tiny thread of resentment. He lit one of his slender brown cigarettes and inhaled deeply, his eyes determinedly fixed on the blazing logs as he drew up his knees and locked his arms loosely around them.

"Don't you think you owe me an explanation?" Alex asked finally, darting her a glance as stormy as black lightning. He took another pull on the cigarette. "Is that cowboy you live with gay?"

"What?" Sabrina said blankly, then swift color pinked her cheeks. This was zooming back to reality with a vengeance. She straightened slowly and drew the drapery about her almost defensively. "No, I don't think I owe you an explanation," she said with equal sharpness. "If you're referring to the fact that I was a virgin, it's no one's business but my own."

"The hell it's not," Alex said roughly, turning to face her and tossing his half-smoked cigarette into the flames. "I regard it as very much my business. It's not every day I make love to a woman I've been given to understand has been living with a man for over two years and find she's green as grass."

"I'm sorry to disappoint you," Sabrina said tartly. "Perhaps your next seduction will live up to your expectations."

"Don't be ridiculous," he said impatiently. "You know very well I nearly went crazy loving you. We were completely fantastic together." He frowned. "It's just that I've run into something that I don't understand at all." His lips tightened. "I don't like not understanding even the tiniest thing about you, Sabrina. It makes me damned nervous. Now what the hell is Bradford to you?"

She smiled sadly. "I told you before, Alex," she said quietly. "I have a commitment to him. I think that's really all you have to know."

"And I told you, you'd have to forget about it." His voice was sharp as a glittering scalpel. "The bond between you can't be all that strong if he was able to keep his hands off you while he was living in the same apartment." His lips twisted. "Two years! I wouldn't have lasted two minutes in the same circumstances! He doesn't have any leaning toward the priesthood by any chance?"

"No," she said wearily. "You don't understand, Alex, and at the moment I don't feel in the mood to make explanations. David is part of my life and there's no reason why you should be allowed to dissect that particular aspect of my existence just because we shared a rather unique physical experience." She drew a deep, steadying breath. "We both know what happened tonight has no real bearing on our everyday lives. We each have our own paths to walk and tomorrow this probably won't even seem real."

"But, it *was* real, damn it," he said moodily, "and I don't agree tonight is an isolated episode out of time. What we had just now, we can have again, and a hell of a lot more. You're crazy if you think this physical chemistry between us is commonplace attraction."

"I don't deny that it's more than that," Sabrina said huskily, glancing away from the burnished copper beauty of his naked figure by the fire. God, this was painful. Each phrase she spoke was tearing at her raw emotions like the flick of a whip. She'd known it would be a mistake to commit her body to Alex in this ultimate physical surrender. Why else had she panicked and run away? Well, the time for running was over. "All I'm saying is that it isn't enough. Sex is all very well and good, and it may be sufficient for the type of relationship you have in mind"—she drew a deep, shaky breath—"but I need more than that, and I don't believe you're capable of giving it."

"I can give you anything in this whole damn world," Alex said roughly. "I told you that before. Name it."

She shook her head, her long lashes lowered to mask her pain. "Will you give me your trust, Alex Ben Raschid?" she asked softly. "Not just for a day or a week, but forever? Will you give me your laughter and your friendship as well as your passion?" She tried to smile. "You see, the price *is* too high for you. And it would be too high for me as well if I found you couldn't meet it after I'd committed myself."

There was a moment of tension-fraught silence. "I'd try," Alex said gruffly, and her gaze flew back to him in surprise. "We've already established that I haven't an overabundance of faith in the human race, but, by God, I'd give it my best shot. As for the other, how can I promise you friendship when all I want to do is come back over there and have you wrap those lovely golden legs around me and bring me home to you." He ignored the little gasp she gave and continued tersely, "Friendship has to grow and you're not willing to give me the time for that growth." His expression was oddly stern. "I don't think you're long on trust yourself, Sabrina."

"Perhaps not," she agreed quietly. "Your actions since the night we first met haven't been calculated to inspire me with that particular emotion. You frightened me." Her eyes met his with a directness that was like a challenge. "But don't think you'll be able to accomplish that feat again, Alex.

I've been acting as insipid and wishy-washy as a mid-Victorian virgin and I assure you it's not my nature to be so meek. Like you, I was caught off guard. I'm usually not so easily intimidated."

There was a flicker of tenderness in the darkness of his eyes and a thread of pride in his voice as he said lightly, "If that's a warning, little flame, then I'm the one that will probably be intimidated. If you're going to display more independence and defiance than you have to date, I'll have my work cut out for me just keeping you from dominating *me*."

Sabrina could feel a reluctant smile tugging at her lips, despite the gravity of the moment. The idea of Alex being dominated by anyone, much less her, was laughable. "I don't think we need worry about that," she said.

"I'm not so sure," he said, frowning. "Now that you have this hold on me, I may have a hell of a lot to worry about."

"Hold?" she asked, her eyes widening in surprise.

His expression had darkened moodily. "I thought I was obsessed by you before, but it's nothing to what I feel now that I've had you. Desire can be a very powerful whip to hold over a man. I don't appreciate your having that kind of power over me."

Sabrina could feel her mouth drop open in surprise before it snapped shut and she glared at him with angry impatience. "For heaven's sake, Alex, could anything illustrate how far we are apart than that asinine remark? I have no intention of wielding any emotional whips and I certainly don't want any so-called power over you. Why don't you just admit there's no possibility of your ever being able to trust me? It would be a great deal less painful for both of us."

"The hell it would!" His dark eyes flickered

angrily. "Okay, so I backslid a little. I said I'd try, not that it would be easy. For God's sake, give me a chance. I told you we need time. *I* need time, blast it!"

"How much time?" Sabrina asked wearily, feeling the aching pain surge through her now that her anger and indignation were ebbing away. "I'm afraid I'm not willing to give you a great deal, Alex. You could hurt me too badly in the interim."

"You may not want to wield the whip but you have quite a natural talent for snapping it, Sabrina," he said dryly. "Will you give me four days to convince you that what we have is worth keeping? It's not as long as I'd like but I think I can make it do."

"Four days," she repeated softly, gazing at him with a yearning tenderness she found impossible to conceal. She had little hope that the time he asked would yield any lasting resolution to their problems. Yet she desperately wanted to wrest those four precious days for herself. Would it be too much to ask for that time with Alex before she once more resumed her responsibilities?

His raking glance read and deciphered that softening, and he moved with swift aggressiveness to take advantage. "Four days," he said coaxingly, his voice like dark velvet over the words. "Give me four days and I promise you'll never want to leave me again, Sabrina. I won't even mention that damn cowboy during the entire time. It'll be just you and me starting out fresh and new. You can teach me to trust, and I'll teach you what that lovely body of yours was meant for."

His glance was a scorching brand as it went over her with lingering thoroughness. Sabrina could feel her breasts swell beneath the cloth she was clutching around her, until the sensitive nipples rubbed with erotic abrasiveness against the material. She felt a hot, melting ache begin to throb in her loins and she shook her head in instinctive rejection as she realized how her body's need was interfering with what should be a coolly logical decision.

Alex evidently mistook her confusion for a negative decision, for his face hardened. "Don't turn me down, Sabrina," he warned with soft menace. "I'm not asking much, but I *will* have those four days!"

"Threats, Alex?" she asked quietly.

"I'm not above using threats if they will get me what I want," he said, his lips tightening. "I don't fool myself that personal threats would have any influence on you, but you're still very vulnerable. There are people out there in your world whom you care about."

He didn't have to say any more. There was that lethal menace about him that Donahue had honed to razor sharpness. "Not a very pleasant way to start a relationship," she said sadly.

"Do you think I wanted to threaten you?" he asked huskily, and, incredibly, there was a flicker of pain in his face. "Don't you know that I want to give you what you need from me? But, damn it, you've got to give me the opportunity to do it!"

"It seems I have little choice," she said. Then she shook her head impatiently. "I'm not being altogether honest, Alex," she said quietly. "I won't pretend to be a victim when I'm nothing of the sort. I would have given you those four days anyway, but you didn't give me the chance, did you?"

"That's very generous of you," he said slowly, and there was no trace of sarcasm in his voice. "Will you be equally honest and admit it's what you want, too?"

"Yes, I'll admit it's what I want," she said faintly.

His eyes were narrowed on her with a hot intimacy that was causing her heart to accelerate and her chest to tighten with emotion. Her tongue ran over her lower lip nervously. "I want *you*, Alex."

Suddenly he was beside her on the cushion. "Then take me, Sabrina," he urged huskily. "Do you know that little pink tongue has darted out and teased the hell out of me at least three times during the past few minutes? I don't think you were even aware of it. My God, what a waste when I'm crazy to have you do that to me." He leaned forward so that their lips were almost brushing. "Give me your tongue, little flame."

Her lips parted and her tongue slowly caressed the full warm curve of his lower lip, before licking hungrily at the corners of his firm mouth like the flame he had called her.

Then Alex's tongue was darting out to touch her own in a hundred glancing kisses that were like an erotic minuet. She felt as if she were on fire, every inch of flesh on her body exquisitely sensitive, even though as yet only their tongues were touching.

Alex's hands were on her shoulders and he was brushing the drapery impatiently aside. One gentle hand was closing around her breast while the other reached between her thighs in a bold assault that robbed her of breath. There was something she had wanted to ask him, but for a moment she couldn't remember what it was through the sensual haze that was enveloping them. Then he was pushing her gently onto her back on the cushions and coming over her with an aroused urgency that caused her to give a little gasp of surprised pleasure.

"Alex," she asked breathlessly. "The four days. Where are we going to spend them?"

"At the moment I'm not at all sure if we'll evei

get away from in front of this fireplace," he muttered thickly, as his lips lowered to nibble teasingly at one engorged nipple. "Let's talk about it later, little flame. Now I want to see you burn for me again."

She was already burning for him, she thought feverishly. He was right, there would be time to talk later. This was the only thing of importance in the universe at the moment. She pulled him down eagerly into her embrace.

Seven

Alex was up before she awoke and had flagged down a Mexican farm worker in an ancient rusty pickup. How he convinced the old man not only to wait until he had brought her from the ranch house, but also to drive them to the Corpus Christi Airport, she could only guess.

He had ignored all her protests against going to the airport in her disheveled condition, that she must contact the Bradfords and Señor Mendoza and let them know she was all right, that she couldn't just fly off blindly to some unknown destination.

"You can call the Bradfords from the airport," he said arrogantly, dispensing with her objections one by one. "Clancy Donahue will contact Mendoza. He's waiting at the Corpus Christi Airport with the Lear jet. You can get everything you need to last you for a few days at the airport shops." He smiled with a teasing intimacy that brought hot color to her cheeks and a boneless melting to her limbs. "You won't need very much. After last night, I may not let you wear a stitch for the entire time I have you in my power, woman."

"That may prove a little embarrassing unless you intend to spend the next few days at a nudist colony," Sabrina said dryly.

He shook his head. "Not a nudist colony," he said, an impish grin lighting the darkness of his face. "Though the idea has definite possibilities." He cocked his head as if pretending to consider. "No, I'd be much too jealous to share your charms with a bunch of gawking strangers. We'll just have to settle for Londale's Folly."

"Londale's Folly?" Sabrina asked blankly.

"It's a private island owned by Sedikhan Petroleum, in the gulf about eighty miles south of Houston," he said briefly. "*Very* private. I have a house there." There was a hint of grimness in the glance he shot her. "I'm not taking any chances of your changing your mind about allotting me my full time with you. You'd find it a bit difficult swimming back to Houston from the Folly."

"Your faith in my word is touching," Sabrina said, with an ironic smile.

"That's what you're supposed to teach me, remember?" he asked lightly.

The pickup was permitted immediate entry by the security officer at the high, wire gate to the field, and chugged directly to the Lear jet at the far end of the tarmac. The pilot, Don Whitehead, opened the door to admit them and didn't bat an eye at Sabrina's rumpled clothing and bare feet when Alex introduced her. Well, why should he, Sabrina thought, knowing a twinge of the green-eyed monster. Piloting a man with Ben Raschid's penchant for lovely bedmates must have accustomed him to seeing a good many women in strange states of dress.

"What's the matter now?" Alex asked impatiently, noticing the tiny frown creasing her forehead after the pilot had retired to the cockpit.

"Nothing," she said quickly. She glanced around the interior of the jet. "This is really quite lovely, Alex."

The furnishings of the plane were sumptuous. The chairs and couch were upholstered in rich cocoa and gold tweed, the walls paneled in mahogany. There was not only a bar at the far end of the cabin but even a tiny kitchen.

Alex pointed to a cream extension telephone resting on a built-in mahogany desk. "You can do your telephoning from here while I go to the terminal and do some shopping for you, then I'll get Clancy working on the arrangements. I'll send catering over to stock the kitchen. Do you have any preferences?"

"Just a sandwich," she said absently, her mind on the difficult call she was about to make.

He nodded briskly. "There's a restroom and shower adjoining the kitchen area if you want to use it. I'll use the VIP facilities at the main terminal." He turned and strode out the door and down the portable metal steps.

Sabrina stared at the phone, biting her lip worriedly, and then reached for the receiver. What the devil was she going to say to Jess and Sue? "Sorry I didn't come home last night, but I was being ravished by a dashing sheik who is whisking me off to his lair for a few more days of dalliance?" Well, she'd come up with something. She drew a deep breath and rapidly punched the Bradford number.

The task turned out to be much easier than she'd expected. It was Jess who picked up the receiver and, after expressing relief at her safety, he listened quietly to her halting explanation that she was going away for a few days.

"I can't say it comes as a surprise, Bree," he said slowly. "The phone lines have been on the fritz since last night, but Juan Mendoza finally got through early this morning. He was a little concerned, to say the least, when both you and this Ben Raschid disappeared without a word. He felt a bit responsible that he'd been manipulated by Ben Raschid into staging the cocktail party. I take it you and Ben Raschid are . . . friends?" The last word was uttered with embarrassed gruffness. "You're sure this is what you want to do?"

"I'm sure," Sabrina said softly. "Tell David I'll be back on Monday and we'll return to Houston the day after." She paused. "Sue did tell you we'd be leaving?"

"She told me," Jess said with a terseness that covered a thread of pain. "It looks like you're still carrying the ball, Bree. It's no wonder you want to run away for a while. God knows we don't have any right to ask what we do of you." He drew a deep, shaky breath. "But I do ask it of you. I have no choice. You will be coming back, won't you, Bree?"

"I'll be back Monday," she repeated gently, her throat aching at the almost pleading note in his voice. "And you're not asking anything of me that I wouldn't do anyway. I made my choice a long time ago, Jess. I love David and there's no way I could desert him now."

"You couldn't say we'd shown it in the last two years, but Sue and I feel you're as much our child as David, Bree," Jess continued bitterly. "We've taken a hell of a lot from you, haven't we? You probably wouldn't be forced to go on this little illicit jaunt with a man like Ben Raschid if you were at liberty to form a more lasting relationship. But what man would be willing to accept the responsibility of a problem like David?"

Sabrina felt a dart of pain so piercing that it took her breath away. She had subconsciously acknowledged a long time ago the truth that Jess stated so frankly, but it had taken on new and poignant meaning since Alex had catapulted into her life. "David's *my* problem," she said shakily. "It wouldn't be fair to ask anyone else to share it." Then she rushed on, her tone firming to deliberate lightness. "Don't worry about it, Jess, it will be years before I'm ready to settle down. By that time we'll probably have David completely well again."

"Maybe," Jess said skeptically. "Bree, are you sure—"

"Look, I've got to hang up now, Jess," Sabrina interrupted, trying to stall off any more of his troubled probing. Though well meant, it was getting a little more painful than she could take at the moment. "Give Sue and David my love. I'll see you Monday."

She replaced the receiver quickly and drew a deep, steadying breath. It was done. Though Jess's words had unintentionally hurt her it was undoubtedly better that she face the reality they encompassed. These four days were all she could expect to have with Alex and she must make the most of them. She would live each day with a zest and joyousness that would make every one a bright jewel to treasure forever. She could do it. If she could gather strength from the darkness, how much more could she garner from the sunlight of this time with Alex?

She rose to her feet and strode to the shower at the rear of the plane.

She was blow-drying her hair with the portable dryer she'd found in a small, compact cabinet under the basin when she heard Alex roaring her name.

"Damn it, where the hell are you, Sabrina?"

She shut off the dryer and frowned in puzzlement. Now what had put him in such a temper?

She tightened the white bath towel around her, tucking the ends beneath her arms.

"Sabrina!"

She slapped the dryer down on the vanity. "I'm coming!" she called, her voice sharp with exasperation. She strode swiftly from the bathroom, her hair flying wildly about her in a flaming, silky cloud. "What's all the urgency?"

Alex halted in mid-stride, a flicker of relief crossing his face before it darkened crossly. "Why didn't you answer before I shouted myself hoarse?" he said roughly, carelessly tossing the armful of packages and the tan pigskin suitcase he was carrying on the seat of a beige contour chair. "And why the hell are you parading around in just a towel? How did you know I was alone?" His lips tightened. "Not that you probably would have minded," he muttered.

"I didn't hear you, I was blow-drying my hair," Sabrina snapped. "And I wouldn't have been parading out here in a towel if you hadn't been bellowing like an angry moose. I thought at the very least the plane must be on fire." She marched over to the chair. "Now if you'll excuse me, I'd like to get dressed. Naturally a shameless slut like me wouldn't feel shyness or modesty, but I am a little chilly."

"Damn, I didn't say you were a slut," he said hoarsely. Then he was behind her, his arms sliding around her and bringing her back against his hard, taut strength. "Why do you put words in my mouth?"

"Close enough," she said, trying desperately to keep her body stiff and unyielding in his arms. The thin terrycloth barrier of the towel might just as well not have been there. She could feel every corded muscle of his hips and thighs against her own rounded softness, and his arms felt beautifully right cradling her so protectively. "And I don't have to put words in your mouth when you do such a superb job of expressing yourself without my help." She tried to wriggle away from him but his arms tightened possessively.

"No," he said sharply, and she could feel his chest move against her back as he took a deep breath. "Don't move, sweetheart. Just let me hold you. Okay?" Then his lips were at her throat, nuzzling aside the silky tresses until they were pressed against the pulse just under her chin. "God, I'm sorry," he muttered thickly. "I know I shouldn't have blown up like that with you. It was just that I was scared half out of my mind. When you didn't answer, I went into a panic."

"Panic?"

"I thought you'd left me," Alex said simply. "I thought your cowboy had talked you into going back to him and you'd cut and run." His next words were muffled against her throat. "Lord, I hate being this vulnerable. It tears me apart."

Sabrina knew a flutter of melting tenderness that had nothing in common with the hot sensuality she'd been aware of only a moment before. She relaxed against him in helpless compliance with the emotional response his words generated. "You're not alone in this, you know," she said huskily. "I can't say that I like what's happened to me either. But I'm not flailing out at you for no reason."

"That's because you're a warm, sweet woman," he said huskily, his lips moving up to her earlobe and nibbling at it gently. "My woman." His tongue darted teasingly into her ear. "Tell me you're my woman, Sabrina?"

"Chauvinist," she charged a trifle breathlessly. She could feel his body hardening against her own and she had a fleeting memory of his powerful, naked body crouched over hers, his supple shoulders gleaming copper in the firelight. She felt a curious weakness in her knees. She shot him a teasing glance from beneath her lashes. "Why don't you tell me you're my man, instead?"

"Why not?" he said mockingly, his hands sliding up to cup the fullness of her breasts through the towel. "I wouldn't think of offending your liberated sensibilities, Sabrina. Particularly when it appears to be nothing less than the truth." His thumbs were lazily stroking her nipples through the rough terry material. "I *am* your man, little flame." She gasped as he increased the abrasive friction that was causing the taut peaks of her breasts to harden yearningly. "Every muscle in my body, every talent I possess, every bit of experience I've acquired over the years are completely at your disposal." His hands slowly pushed the towel down to her waist and thumb and forefinger were gently plucking at the nipples he'd already aroused to such excruciating sensitivity. "Tell me what you want, love," he urged softly, his warm breath stirring the hair at her temples. "Tell your man how he can please you."

One hand left her breast to wander down to the apex of her thighs, and he began a lazy, circular, rubbing motion through the towel. She shivered as she felt a hot wave of unadulterated desire rock her. "Do you like that, sweetheart? Do you know how much I like to touch you there? You're so soft and sweet." His hand increased its stroking tempo until she was arching instinctively against it, her eyes closing against the tide of pleasure he was causing to break over her. "So hot."

"Alex." His name was almost a gasp on her lips and suddenly she couldn't take any more. She turned in his arms and her trembling fingers were at the buttons of his shirt. "Damn you, Alex. Liberated, hell! You know you're driving me crazy."

There was a flicker of mischief in the darkness of his eyes, despite the pulse she could see leaping in his throat, signaling his own arousal. "Well, I didn't actually *know*," he drawled, smiling. "I admit I did have a strong hunch, though." He raised an eyebrow quizzically as she pulled his shirt out of his pants and parted the material, baring his muscular chest with its springy pelt of dark hair. "Does that mean you don't want to be liberated any more?" He pulled a face. "Pity. I was just beginning to enjoy my submissive role."

Submissive? Sabrina gave a very unladylike snort of disbelief. She should have known better than to try to play games with Alex. He had too much experience on his side, and that inborn arrogance was a little too strong to allow him to yield anyone a total victory. Or was it?

"You like aggressive women, then?" she asked sweetly, her eyes narrowed thoughtfully on his face. "I'll have to see if I can't accommodate you." She leaned forward and deliberately rubbed her naked breasts against the hard muscles of his chest. The mockery was abruptly wiped from his face. "Do you like that, sweetheart?" she asked with dulcet sweetness, parodying his own seductive whisper. "Do you know how much I like to touch you there?" She bent her head and her tongue darted out to caress one hard male nipple. He groaned this time and his hips gave a spasmodic jerk forward. She looked up into his eyes and crooned soulfully, "You're *so* hot."

For a moment he gazed down at her in blank disbelief. Then suddenly he was chuckling. He threw back his head and laughed with such robust enjoyment that it was her turn to stare at him blankly.

His arms went around her and he gave her a warm, affectionate hug that was almost avuncular. "Oh Lord, Sabrina, there's no one like you," he said, still chuckling. He pressed her head to his chest, rocking her back and forth like a proud parent with his favorite child. "Just when I think I've gotten the best of you, you do something like this. It'll be a wonder if I have the least bit of ego left by the time these four days are over."

"I don't think you have to worry too much about that," Sabrina said dryly. "I haven't exactly noticed you've turned into a shrinking violet since I came on the scene." But her arms slipped around his waist beneath his shirt and she brushed a light kiss on the warm flesh cushioning her cheek. God, she loved him so much. How could you help but love a man who could subdue his pride, and laugh at himself, without losing one particle of the essence that made him all strong, virile male?

There was a sound somewhere between a snort and a cough behind her. Sabrina stiffened and made an instinctive movement to turn and face the new arrival on the scene, an action instantly quelled by Alex's arms tightening about her protectively. It was a good thing he had, she realized an instant later, embarrassed color flooding her face. Naked to the waist, with only a flimsy towel draping her hips, she was scarcely presentable.

"Shall I go out and come in again?" Clancy Donahue asked politely.

"You have abominable timing, Clancy." Alex sighed resignedly over her head to Donahue standing at the door. He carefully folded the edge of his shirt around Sabrina's naked back, affording her a little more covering. "Do you intend to make a habit of this?"

"You're obviously not going to give me the opportunity." Donahue's voice was laden with displeasure. "I made those arrangements you ordered. You know what a damn fool you're being, don't you?"

"Not now, Clancy," Alex said impatiently. "Go on up to the cockpit and give Sabrina a chance to get dressed. You're embarrassing her."

There was a disgruntled murmur behind her and then the soft click of the cockpit door. She raised her head from Alex's chest, her cheeks still flaming. "I don't think you need to worry about my appearing draped only in a towel any more," she said ruefully. "That was the second time I've been embarrassed to death by Clancy's arrival."

Swift concern darkened his face. "I wanted you to be discreet, not ashamed." His hands left her back to cup her face in his palms. "You shouldn't ever be ashamed of that lovely body, little flame," he said softly. "You're all glowing satin color and singing grace." He kissed her with a tenderness that caused her to catch her breath. "If I sometimes get uptight about you displaying all that magic to anyone else, it's just because I'm a jealous bastard and like to guard my own. Okay?"

"Okay," she answered throatily. She smiled shakily. "Now I think I'd better put some clothes on, don't you? Clancy must think I'm trying to establish going topless as the current fashion."

He released her reluctantly and stepped back, watching as she pulled the towel up to cover her breasts and tightened it around her. "It's not a half-bad idea," he said wistfully, his eyes on her cleavage. Then he pulled his gaze forcibly away and grinned mockingly. "And Clancy would never hint you'd ever do anything that wasn't entirely right and proper. He's a great fan of yours." His lips tightened grimly. "He's a little too enthusiastic in his support of you at times. Did you know he tried to talk me out of coming to Corpus Christi to get you once I'd located you? It's the first time since I was a kid that I was tempted to take a swing at him. What the hell did he think I was going to do to you?"

"Probably exactly what you did," Sabrina said, her lips curving in amusement. She felt a warm surge of affection for the gruff Texan. "He knows you very well, Alex." She turned briskly back to the chair and started to gather up the packages. "How much time do I have to get dressed before we take off?"

"About fifteen minutes," he said absently, still frowning. He watched her broodingly as she turned back toward the bathroom. "How did I know you were a virgin?" he said defensively, looking like a sulky little boy.

"Would it have made any difference?" she asked over her shoulder as she crossed the cabin. Why was he so upset by Donahue's championing of her? It seemed completely out of character in someone as ruthlessly single-minded as Alex.

His lips curved in a reluctant smile. "Probably not," he admitted sheepishly. "I wanted you too much to give a damn about anything!" His expression became oddly grave. "I guess I just resent the fact that Clancy felt he had to protect you from me. I want to be the one to protect you from anything that could hurt you."

"Cherish?" Sabrina asked softly, as she paused at the door and gazed at him across the cabin.

"Cherish," he echoed. There was a touch of uncertainty in the depths of his eyes and lines of tension about his mouth. "I didn't just take a lush little redhead I had a yen for to bed last night, Sabrina. I think you know that despite what Clancy thinks. Are you sorry you let me love you?"

How could she be sorry? It had been the most

wildly beautiful experience of her entire life. Whatever was to come afterward, that fact was incontestable. Her emerald eyes were glowing with tenderness as she said huskily, "You've got to get rid of these chauvinistic misconceptions if we're ever to understand each other, Alex. I didn't *let* you love me, I demanded it. I wouldn't think of accepting such a passive role. Keep that in mind in the future." The door closed softly behind her.

In fifteen minutes she was dressed in the cream Halston pants suit with its chic tunic top and graceful, cowl neck. The matching medium-heel sandals were not only fashionable but marvelously comfortable. For that matter everything fit splendidly, she thought with satisfaction. Alex had been almost uncannily accurate in his guesses regarding her sizes. Then she felt a swift surge of heat flood her entire body at the memory of the events of the previous night. It wasn't all that amazing when she came to think about it. In those feverishly passionate hours before they had finally fallen into an exhausted slumber, he must have weighed and measured every inch of her, not only with his eyes but with those talented hands and those lips that had practically driven her out of her mind.

There was still a flush of color on her cheeks as she returned to the cabin and found it unoccupied except for Clancy Donahue, sprawled lazily in an easy chair, leafing through a magazine. He rose easily to his feet, his brows raised and his lips pursed in an appreciative whistle as his gaze ran over her.

"Very nice," he said lightly, his blue eyes twinkling. "I found the other outfit a bit more aesthetically pleasing, but a man can't have everything." Then as her blush deepened to a color rivaling her hair, he added more soberly, "Sorry about that. I promised Alex I wouldn't say anything to embarrass you, but he should have known I wouldn't be able to resist. This unruly tongue of mine has been landing me in trouble since I was a lad. Speaking of exotic outfits, I have something that belongs to you." He reached into the pocket of his tweed sports jacket, pulled out a cassette tape, and held it out to her. "You forgot this the night of Alex's birthday party. I suppose I could have mailed it to you but I had an idea I'd be seeing you again very soon anyway." His eyes twinkled. "I just didn't think I'd be seeing so *much* of you."

"Thank you," she said quickly, taking the tape. She sat down in the chair next to his. "Where is Alex?"

Donahue nodded in the direction of the cockpit. "He decided to take over the controls himself since it's only a forty-minute flight to Houston International. You'll be changing to the helicopter there. Londale's Folly doesn't have a landing strip. He usually prefers to have Don take over on longer flights so he can rest or work as the mood takes him." He smiled. "Of course it could be that he decided discretion was the better part of valor, with a lovely thing like you sharing the cabin. I got the distinct impression he wasn't up to exercising much more restraint where you were concerned, and he practically burned my ears off for the embarrassment I'd already caused you."

"I'm sorry. That was quite unfair," she murmured. "It wasn't your fault I was embarrassed."

"I totally agree! But that didn't stop Alex from blistering me with that poison tongue of his. Sometimes I rue the day I taught him my rather uniquely explicit vocabulary." He scowled. "I only wish he'd picked up a grain or two of common sense along with it."

"I gather you're a trifle displeased with him," she said idly, as she fastened her seat belt. "I seem to remember your calling Alex a fool. That's hardly the action of the poor, downtrodden employee you're picturing yourself to be."

Donahue's face darkened grimly. "He is a fool," he repeated stubbornly. "He knows better than to take chances in his position. It's the first time I've ever known him to take a risk for no good reason." He glared at her resentfully. "I'd say it's carrying your desire for privacy a little too far, risking Alex's life just to spare yourself a little publicity, Sabrina."

"Risking Alex's life?" Sabrina's eyes were wide with surprise and questioning. "I don't have any idea what you're talking about, Clancy."

He studied her for a long moment before the skepticism slowly faded from his face. "I should have known it was all Alex's idea," he said gruffly. "Forget I mentioned it, kid."

"Forget you mentioned it?" Sabrina said, staring at him incredulously. "You've just accused me of putting Alex's life in danger and now you want me to forget it?"

"It would be a hell of a lot more comfortable for me if you would," he said gloomily. "Alex is going to tear a strip off me for even bringing it up."

"Clancy, will you stop this waffling and tell me what you meant?" Sabrina was practically seething with frustration. "Why is Alex's life in danger?"

"I didn't say his life was actually in danger," he said defensively, "just that he was stupid to take the chance." Then, as she drew a long, exasperated breath he continued reluctantly, "Alex has given orders that for the next four days you're to be totally alone on Londale's Folly. He doesn't want any of his security force even to set foot on the island. He had me send the housekeeper and handyman to the mainland for your stay there."

He scowled in disgust. "Did you ever hear anything so crazy in your life?"

Sabrina could feel the tension flow out of her like the air from a pricked balloon. My God, what a tempest in a teapot. He'd frightened her half to death. "Is that all?" she asked, with a profound sigh of relief. "Clancy Donahue, if you ever do that to me again, it's you whose life will be in danger!"

"Is that all?" Donahue echoed grimly. "I assure you that it's quite enough! Would it interest you to know that there have been three attempts on Alex's life since he came of age? And four kidnapping attempts? Why do you think he maintains a security force that rivals the U.S. Secret Service?"

"I didn't know he did," Sabrina said faintly. She suddenly felt icy cold. "Why would anyone want to kill Alex?"

"Oh, for heaven's sake, Sabrina! Because he's Alex Ben Raschid, of course," Donahue said wearily. "You can't wield that much power without stepping on a few toes along the way. Not to mention his position as the next ruler of Sedikhan. Old Karim has been ill lately and it's just a matter of time until Alex takes total control there as well. It's only logical that any group hoping to topple Alex's family from power would pick a time like now to do it. If anything, security should be tightened, not eliminated entirely as Alex is doing, on the island."

"I see," Sabrina said slowly. She moistened her suddenly dry lips. "Then of course that's what you'll have to do. I have no objection to security men on the island. I'm sure Alex will change his mind when you tell him how urgent you feel the arguments are for their being there."

"Fat chance," Donahue said ruefully. "Alex

doesn't do anything he doesn't want to and it's obvious he wants to keep you very much to himself." Then, as his keen eyes raked over her pale, strained face, he reached out and covered her hand, giving it a firm, reassuring squeeze. "Don't worry, hon, I'll find a way of protecting him, even if it means anchoring the yacht offshore and ringing the Folly with a small flotilla!"

She bit her lip. "You're sure?" She felt a surge of almost fierce protectiveness, along with chilling panic, at the thought of Alex in danger. Nothing could happen to Alex. She wouldn't let it. It was ironic that both David and Alex, whom she loved in such different ways, should be able to inspire this same maternal ferocity.

"I'm very sure," he said comfortingly. "And don't forget, in the general run of events Alex is more than capable of taking care of himself. I made damn sure of that."

"That's right, you did," Sabrina answered, the tight coil of fear loosening a trifle. "Thank God for that!" She gave him a grateful smile. "And thank *you* for keeping him safe all these years, Clancy."

His blunt face was gentle as he gazed at her searchingly for a long moment. "So the running is all over."

"Yes, the running is over," she answered simply. "I never should have bolted in the first place. I told you it wasn't my way."

"I hope it works out for you, kid," Clancy said softly, his blue eyes kind.

There was a mellow ping and the seat-belt light glowed over the cockpit door. It was followed immediately by the whine of the jet engines. Donahue hurriedly fastened his seat belt and checked Sabrina's before settling back in his chair.

"We have forty minutes," he said, a curious

smile on his face. "I think that should be just about enough time for me to tell you about a fascinating place I have a hunch you'll be visiting soon. It's a country that's half space-age technology and half Arabian-nights fairy tale. It's a land called Sedikhan and the first time I saw it I said to myself . . ."

Eight

"This is your room," Alex said briskly, throwing open the door and preceding Sabrina into a guest room with lush, deep, sea-blue carpet. He crossed to the double bed in the center of the room and tossed onto the aqua satin spread the small suitcase containing the clothes he'd purchased at the airport. "I'm just down the hall in the master suite." He cast a glance at the gold watch on his wrist. "It's only a little after four. Would you like to go for a walk and explore the island a bit before we scrounge in the kitchen for something for dinner?"

"What?" she asked, bewildered. *Her* room? She'd assumed they'd be sharing a room. Alex certainly hadn't impressed her as the type of man who'd be content to occupy his own bed and visit her when the mood struck him. He was much too possessive. "Oh, yes, that would be very nice," she agreed politely.

"Fine," he said tersely, not looking at her as he turned and strode quickly to the door as if eager to escape. "Suppose I meet you downstairs in fifteen minutes then?" The door closed behind him.

She stared blankly at the door for a long moment before she moved slowly toward the bed, opened the pigskin suitcase, and pulled out a pair of white shorts and a yellow cotton suntop. What on earth was the matter? Alex had acted so cold and had practically run out the door.

Now that she thought about it, he'd been curiously remote and stilted from the moment they'd changed aircraft at Houston. She really hadn't noticed it at the time, assuming he was just absorbed in the mechanics of flying the helicopter. Then, too, she'd been excited at her first glimpse of this lovely, tropical island and the enchanting hillside villa built entirely of gleaming gray stone. But there was no doubt in her mind now that something was definitely wrong. Alex's cool rejection of her had been far from subtle.

As she automatically stripped off the cream pants suit and dressed in the shorts and suntop, her mind gnawed at his strange behavior. It just didn't make sense. She couldn't believe Alex could change so radically from the passionate lover of this morning. She scoffed at the very notion that the thrill of the chase was over and he could have lost interest. She thrust her feet into white strappy sandals. Alex's mood was totally incomprehensible.

Her expression must have reflected her uncertainty and dismay when she came down the stairs, for Alex's face darkened in an impatient frown as he stood in the foyer watching her. "You're looking at me as if I were Bluebeard incarnate," he said roughly. His glance went over the snug white shorts and low-cut blouse moodily. "And you haven't got on enough clothes."

Sabrina's mouth fell open and for an instant she could only gape at him. "It must be almost ninety degrees outside, and if you'll recall, you're the one who chose my entire wardrobe for our stay on the island." She crossed her arms over her chest and glared at him belligerently. "Which, I might add, seems to be comprised principally of very scanty shorts and tops and a bikini that would make a Bourbon Street stripper blush."

"I know," he said gloomily. "I chose them before I decided . . ." His voice trailed off. "Oh hell, I guess you'll have to wear them." He grabbed her elbow and hustled her hurriedly toward the front door. "Come on, I'll show you around the island."

If she'd had any thoughts of a leisurely amble around this tropical paradise, she would have been rudely disillusioned. Alex behaved as if he were in training for the Boston Marathon as he bustled her out of the house and down the palm-bordered path to the beach. He gave her a brief and concise history of the island, lending it all the color of a stock report. The only time he allowed her to stop was to examine the exterior of the small, stone cottage in the cove, which, he told her, Honey and Lance Rubinoff occupied when they visited the island. Even then he flatly refused to allow her to enter the cottage, and the marathon was on again.

By the time they returned to the house, Sabrina's cheeks were flushed, not only by the sun and their rapid pace but in angry exasperation. There was no possible excuse for Alex to behave so churlishly. When he showed every indication of continuing his sterile, guidebook tour in the house, starting with the terrace, she decided she'd had enough.

She skidded to an abrupt stop and jerked her elbow away from his firm hold. "Okay, Alex, I've had it!" She marched to the gray stone balustrade bordering the flagstone terrace and levered herself so that she was sitting on the wide ledge. She planted her hands firmly on her hips. "I'll be damned if I'll stand you treating me as if I were some kind of plague victim. If you've changed your mind about wanting me here, you only have to say so. I don't need any demonstration like the one you've just put me through."

"I don't know what you're talking about," he said, frowning like a sulky little boy. "You said you wanted to see the island."

"Don't play dense, Alex," Sabrina gritted between clenched teeth. "We both know you've been acting very peculiarly since we arrived on the island."

"Maybe a little," he admitted moodily. "Give me a little time and I'll get a handle on it."

"Alex, we only have four days," she protested impatiently. "What in the world is wrong with you?"

He was across the terrace in four swift strides. "Damn it, this is what's wrong!" He grabbed her hand and brought it to his steel-hard arousal and held it there. "I want you. I'm aching like hell and it's promising to be a permanent state of affairs where you're concerned."

An instant of shock was quickly superseded by relief that made her almost weak with reaction. Good Lord, was that all? Her hand gently moved over the warm hard length of him. "I don't see anything wrong there," she said softly, her other hand moving to the buttons of her suntop. "Why didn't you tell me? I think we can take care of that problem fairly easily."

He closed his eyes, his hips thrusting forward against her hand and his lean face taut with an almost pained delight. "Sabrina, don't do that," he choked hoarsely. "You're killing me."

If it was killing him, it was with pleasure, Sabrina thought tenderly, noticing the color suffuse the bronze darkness of his cheeks. He was so beautiful like this, with a look on his face that was so strong, yet oddly vulnerable. Her hand moved in a more aggressive caress and he gave a groan, quickly followed by a shudder through his entire body. "Sabrina!"

Then he was jerking desperately away from her, his eyes flicking open. He hurriedly drew back from her as if she really did have the plague. "No, damn it!" he said emphatically. "I'm not going to do it. Stay away from me, Sabrina!" His dark gaze was drawn compulsively to her breasts which were almost entirely revealed by the half-buttoned suntop. "And cover up!"

"You seem to be saying that to me quite a lot," Sabrina said bewilderedly, her hands automatically drawing the blouse closed. "At this rate, you're going to give me a complex."

"And you're going to drive me stark, staring insane," Alex said, drawing a deep breath. "I'm definitely not made for the celibate life."

"Celibate?" Sabrina asked dazedly. "Who's asking you to be celibate? What about all those lovely things you were going to teach me?"

"I changed my mind," he said tersely, and then, as her eyes widened in disbelief, he continued quickly, "only for the next couple of days." His lips twisted wryly. "I don't think I can hold out any longer than that."

"Why would you want to hold out at all?" she asked blankly. "There can't be any question in your mind about my willingness on that score."

There was a glint of warm tenderness in Alex's eyes. "No, I've no doubt about you, love. You're the most beautifully responsive woman I've ever known."

"Then why?"

"It's *because* we're so damn good together," he said simply. "Like I said, I seem to be in a permanent state of arousal whenever I so much as have a fleeting thought about you. The minute I take you to bed, there's every possibility we'd spend the rest of the time together making love." He shook his head, his lips tightening. "Pleasurable as that might be for both of us, at the end of four days you'd get out of that bed and walk away. The only things I'd have taught you about me and about yourself would be purely physical. I can't afford that, Sabrina."

"So it's celibacy for both of us?" She chuckled, her eyes dancing. Alex's struggle to keep himself from taking her most definitely had a funny side. Then her smile faded, to be replaced with a poignant tenderness. No, it wasn't funny at all. It was sweet and tender and a little sad.

"Until we establish those other levels of communication you said were so important to you," he said sternly. "And no amount of seduction on your part is going to change my mind."

"I told you this morning you weren't alone in this," she said gently, her face glowing with a loving tenderness that caused the man watching her to inhale sharply. "Why won't you believe me? Instead of treating me as if I were an enemy out to undermine you, why couldn't you just discuss it with me? You know, I believe your reasoning seems quite sound."

His dark eyes flickered warily. "You do?"

"I do," she answered softly. Much as she hated the thought of any postponement of her physical relations with Alex, there was something very appealing in the idea. She would learn all she could of this multidimensional man, whose personality seemed to be gradually capturing every corner of her heart.

"And if you'd told me the problem, I would have helped," she added. "That's what caring is all about. Don't you know that?"

"I haven't had much experience in that area,"

Alex answered, his gaze intent on her face. "Perhaps you can teach me that, too."

"Perhaps."

If example could teach him, then Alex should prove a very good student, she thought mistily. Sometimes the love she felt for him seemed to be literally radiating out from her, like a glowing sun.

She slipped from the balustrade to the flagstone terrace, her hands swiftly buttoning her blouse. "Now, if we're to start off this platonic friendship properly, it would be a good idea if I got out of these clothes. Where did you say your bedroom was? Oh yes, just down the hall from mine."

"My bedroom?" he asked blankly.

She chuckled. "Don't worry, Alex, I'm not about to force myself into your bed. I just thought I'd raid your closet and try to find something to wear that was a little less revealing than these clothes." She crossed the few feet separating them and gave him a light, loving kiss on the lips. "You see, there's no way I'd ever want you aching or uncomfortable even if it's with desire for me." She kissed him again. "And that's caring, too!" She turned and walked swiftly toward the French doors that led to the lounge.

"Sabrina."

She turned at the door, her eyes inquiring.

"Do you play chess?" Alex's expression was so beautifully tender that at first she couldn't pull her gaze away from it to comprehend his words.

Then she frowned in puzzlement. "Not very well. I don't really have the sort of logical mind it requires. Checkers are more my game. Why?"

"I just thought we should have something to occupy us for the next two days," he said, smiling.

"Checkers it is, then." As she turned once more to

the door his voice was a husky murmur behind her. "Thank you, Sabrina."

"For what?" she asked over her shoulder.

"For caring, love, for caring."

"Alex, just one more," Sabrina pleaded. "I haven't got any shells with this lovely lavender pink. One more won't hurt."

"That's what you said about the sand dollar," Alex said, trying to frown sternly at her. "You must have gathered at least two hundred shells this afternoon. Why do you have to have that one?"

"But this one has such a beautiful—"

He held up his hand. "Okay, okay." He untied their makeshift knapsack and gestured resignedly. "Throw it in with the rest. I must be getting soft. Not only do I let you take the shirt off my back to carry your loot, but I find myself conned by a red-haired brat who has all the appeal of Huckleberry Finn."

"Huckleberry Finn was very appealing," Sabrina protested, placing the shell in the knapsack and watching contentedly as Alex once more knotted the ends. "He's my favorite Mark Twain character. He had such a spirit of adventure." She made a face as she looked down at her less-than-elegant apparel, comprised of a pair of Alex's jeans she'd rolled up to her knees to wade in the surf, and a blue shirt whose tails were flapping about her thighs. "I can see your point though." She sighed ruefully. "I think I may have gone overboard on toning down my sex appeal. You'd have to be a child molester to see anything attractive about me at the moment."

He straightened and slung the bundle over his shoulder, his muscles rippling like burnished copper in the late afternoon sunlight. "Oh, I don't know," he drawled, his dark eyes twinkling. He reached out and gave her ponytail a teasing little tug. "You definitely have something you didn't have when we arrived at the island day before yesterday."

"I do?" Sabrina asked warily. She'd discovered that at times Alex could exhibit an almost puckish sense of humor. "And what is that?"

"Three freckles across the bridge of your nose," he said, touching one with the tip of his finger. "And a better knowledge of the game of checkers."

"*I* was the one who was conned," Sabrina sputtered indignantly. "You didn't tell me you were a damn expert at the game. And then you had the nerve to play me for kitchen duty. Is that any way to treat a guest?"

"I can't cook," Alex said logically, lacing his fingers through hers and automatically shortening his stride as they turned back toward the path that led uphill to the villa. "It was better for both of us that you take over in that department. Besides, I consider I'm being very generous to help you with the washing-up when that was included in the wager."

"Very generous," Sabrina said ironically. She darted him a curious glance. "Where did you learn to play checkers anyway?"

"Clancy."

"I should have known." She sighed resignedly. "No wonder you win all the time. Clancy would make sure there wasn't a chance of your not coming out on top in any passage at arms." Her gaze raked the horizon. "Is he really out there somewhere? I haven't seen any sign of the yacht all the time we've been here."

"Knowing Clancy, you can be sure of it," Alex said dryly. "He's as worry prone as a hypochondriac in a leper colony." His expression darkened grimly. "And the reason you haven't seen the yacht is that he knows I'd have his hide if you did. I'll be damned if I'll have him frightening you off."

"I'm glad he's out there," Sabrina said soberly, her hand tightening involuntarily in his. "I wish you'd let him stay at the cottage. I don't like you to take chances, Alex."

"There's very little risk," he said carelessly. "As I said, Clancy just likes to fuss." He raised an eyebrow as he glanced down at her troubled face. "But I'm glad you're concerned. It shows I'm making progress. Maybe my monklike abstinence is being rewarded, after all." He made a face. "I certainly hope so. I'm finding the path of virtue strewn with thorns despite the fact that I'm trodding it with Huckleberry Finn."

She stopped and turned to face him, her expression grave. "Has it been bad for you, Alex?" she asked, a tiny frown knitting her forehead. "I thought you were enjoying yourself." She could feel the foolish tears misting her eyes and blinked them away determinedly. "I've loved every minute of it."

"And so have I," Alex said gently, then noticing the liquid emerald of her eyes gazing up at him uncertainly, he muttered an extremely blue imprecation. "Now I've hurt you!" he said impatiently, running his fingers through his hair. "Why do redheads have to be so emotional?"

"Don't generalize," Sabrina said, her lips trembling. "I'm not one of your harem of redheads. I'm me, Sabrina Courtney."

"A very emotional Sabrina Courtney," Alex said gruffly. "But you're right, I should be the last one to complain. You can't be too emotional to suit me, sweetheart."

"Make up your mind, Alex," Sabrina said, trying

to free her hand from his grip. "You're being contradictory!"

"Because, as usual, I seem to have put my foot in my mouth," Alex said ruefully. "I suppose I should be used to it now with you. It's been that way ever since the moment we met." He took her arm and propelled her toward a palm-shaded hillock several yards away. "Come on, we're going to talk. I'm not about to let a misunderstanding rear its ugly head at this stage of the game."

When they reached the palm trees, he dropped the bundle to the ground. Placing both hands on her arms, he pushed her gently to her knees. "Sit down," he said, "this may take quite a while." He sank to his knees facing her and settled back on his heels. "Now, be still and let me try to explain myself, okay?"

"Okay," Sabrina replied, gazing blindly over his shoulder at the gentle roll of the surf.

"Look at me, please," he asked, before cradling her face in his hands. "Stay with me, Sabrina. This is the first time since we came to the Folly that you've gone away from me somewhere I can't follow. Come back to me, sweetheart." His hard face softened with a luminous tenderness. "I'm lonely for you."

"Are you, Alex?" she asked uncertainly. The world had narrowed to his dark intent face so close to her own. "I wasn't sure."

"Then be sure," he said softly, his fingers moving upward to caress the delicate skin of her temples with mesmerizing gentleness. "When I suggested this little platonic hiatus, I fully expected it to be hell on earth. I thought I'd be roasting on hot coals the entire time. Shall I tell you what I found instead?"

She nodded slowly, her eyes fixed almost hypnotically on his dark ones that seemed to encompass all that was loving and caring in the world.

"I found a companion I'd want beside me if we were stranded on this island for the next hundred years. I found a woman who is half pixie, half tomboy, and still manages to be all woman." His voice was so low it was almost a whisper but it rang with a sincerity that caused her throat to tighten painfully. "I found the other half of me. Sometimes I feel as if we're so close I could read your mind." He shook his head, his lips curving in a rueful smile. "It would probably be better if you could read mine. It would prevent a good many misunderstandings."

"You're not the easiest man in the world to understand, Alex," she said huskily. "The first time I saw your portrait I thought you looked like a man who knew more secrets than the Sphinx."

"Do you think I don't know how I shut people away from me?" he asked quietly. "But I haven't closed myself away from you, Sabrina. The gates were rusty and creaky with disuse, but I've held them open and let you take a look. I don't think you've seen any dark secrets to send you running away in panic."

She shook her head. "No, the man I've seen hasn't frightened me, Alex," she said softly. "I like him very much."

She liked him far too much. There had been moments in the last two days when she'd felt she'd made a terrible mistake in allowing this time of exploration and discovery between them. Her body might someday forget the witchery they knew together, but how was her mind to make a similar adjustment, now that she'd discovered the man behind the mask? The wry humor that was always just beneath that enigmatic surface, and the gossamer gentleness that could emerge so unexpectedly from the tough shell he'd built around himself. The other half of him. Yes, she'd felt that ephemeral bond and known it was gaining strength with each passing moment. When their stay on the island was over, would she find it too hard to break?

"Good, I'm glad you like me," he said gruffly. "Remember that. There's going to come a time when I'll remind you that you found something besides my virile young body fascinating." He frowned with mock sternness. "So, from now on, don't get any crazy ideas just because I drop the casual, lustful remark." He sighed. "I'm sorry, love. I appreciate the effort, but you could be wrapped in sackcloth and ashes and I'd still want you." He kissed her lightly on the tip of her nose. "But that doesn't mean I don't like having my Huckleberry Finn around." There was suddenly a glint of mischief in the darkness of his eyes. "Especially as young Huck owes me kitchen duty again tonight, and I haven't had anything to eat since breakfast."

"Philistine," Sabrina accused, jumping to her feet. The moment was so charged with emotion she felt a swift rush of relief that Alex had chosen to lighten it. They had been much too close to words that mustn't be spoken. "If you promise to wash all my shells for me, I just might oblige, despite the way you hustled me."

He retrieved the knapsack and weighed it consideringly. "No deal," he said, standing up and slinging it over his shoulder. "It would take me the better part of the evening and I have other plans for tonight."

"Plans?" Sabrina asked, as he took her hand and their steps once more turned toward the path.

"I said I could last two days," he reminded her quietly. "And I think I accomplished what I set out to do. You can't deny we know each other better now than some couples who have been married for years."

Sabrina felt a little tingle of heat surge through her and she unconsciously licked her lips in anticipation. She knew she'd been eagerly waiting this decision, though she hadn't admitted it even to herself. They'd made the attempt to dampen down the explosive sexuality that was ever present between them, still the undercurrents had been unmistakable. Now the waiting was almost over. She'd be in Alex's arms tonight.

"No, I can't deny we know each other better," she agreed softly, casting him a sideways glance redolent with mischief. "But I'll be darned if I'll play both roles you seem to require of me, Alex Ben Raschid. If you want a mistress in your bed tonight, the kitchen slave has to go!"

When they reached the house, Alex proceeded directly to the suite to shower and change while Sabrina continued on to the small utility room adjoining the modern kitchen. She'd put a load of clothes in the dryer before they'd started out on their walk this afternoon, and she wanted to fold and return them to Alex's room before she went to her own room to change. Since she'd been sharing Alex's wardrobe for the past two days, it had been necessary to wash clothes frequently.

A happy smile tugged at the corners of her mouth as she folded the jeans and shirts when she took them out of the dryer. It would be good to get back into clothes that made her look a bit more alluring than the ones she had on now. Wearing his may have been both practical and discreet, but it had chafed at her pride to know she wasn't at her best with Alex. Heavens, it was natural for a woman to want to be beautiful for the man she loved.

She was mentally going over the neglected wardrobe in her closet as she gathered up the neat pile of clothes. There was a silky polyester blouse in a nile green shade that might look rather good with her eyes. She climbed the stairs and strode briskly down the hall to the master suite at the end of the corridor.

Alex didn't answer her perfunctory knock and, when she opened the door, the sound of the shower running in the adjoining bathroom supplied the reason. She crossed to a teak bureau against the far wall and cast an admiring, proprietal glance around the large, lovely room.

Like the rest of the decor of the house, it had a vaguely tropical atmosphere, with a thick shag carpet in a variegated blue green, the exact shade of the sea she'd been playing in a short time ago. One wall was entirely comprised of a sliding, louvered closet in a rich, polished teak, and there was an elegant empress chair beside the king-sized bed.

After the first glance at that massive bed she carefully avoided looking at it. There were too many hours to get through before she could afford to visualize Alex making love to her there.

She briskly opened the top drawer of the teak bureau and put in two pairs of jeans. Now had Alex taken these T-shirts from the second or third drawer? The second, she decided, and pulled open the drawer.

The pale blue nightgown was so sheer that it was a mere drift of cobweb chiffon, and for a moment she just stared at it with a queer sense of shock. Then she reached out with a careful hand to lift the beautiful thing from the drawer. Judging by the size, the owner must be an exceptionally voluptuous woman, she thought numbly. The nightgown fell from her fingers in a pool of color and she couldn't take her eyes off it. It exerted the same deadly fascination as a lovely coral snake and she felt as if she'd been stung with a poison that was just as nerve paralyzing.

Oh God, why did it hurt so much to know that Alex had made love to another woman in this very room, in that bed? Everyone who could read a newspaper knew Alex changed mistresses with a rapidity that was positively dizzying. Why wouldn't he bring one of them to this island? And why couldn't she accept it like a mature, sophisticated woman instead of feeling like a betrayed child?

The pain was almost comparable to the agony she'd known at the Mendoza party, when he'd spoken with such callous ruthlessness of the women he'd taken. Yet that reality seemed to be of another world. It didn't belong on this island with the man who'd carried her shells over his shoulder and teased her about her freckles. The very closeness they'd attained in the last two days made the intrusion seem even more foreign. He was hers, damn it!

"Moving in?" Alex asked casually. He was leaning indolently against the doorjamb of the bathroom. "I thoroughly approve. We'll be much more comfortable in here than in your room." He leered with mock lasciviousness. "I can't wait to show you the sunken bathtub. It's almost as large as one of the guest rooms."

She must have been staring at that nightgown longer than she'd realized, she thought absently. Alex was dressed in close-fitting khakis that intimately molded the strong, muscular line of his thighs. The sleeves of his dark brown sport shirt were rolled up casually to the elbow, revealing his bronze forearms. He'd even had time to neatly comb his hair that was still damp from the shower.

He came to her and dropped a light kiss on the

nape of her neck. Sabrina was vaguely aware of the clean fragrance of soap and a light woodsy cologne. He reached around her and with a disapproving frown picked up the blue chiffon gown from the open drawer. "I don't remember choosing this for you." He dropped it back into the drawer. "It must have been temporary insanity. There's no way I'm going to let even that little bit of mist come between us tonight." His arms slid around her and he drew her back against the warm length of his body.

"You did include a nightgown in the wardrobe you gave me," she said tightly, "but this isn't it. I've never seen this one before."

"No?" His lips moved up to nibble at her ear. "Then it must be Honey's, she wears that shade of blue quite a bit."

"I thought you said Honey and Lance always used the cottage when they were here," Sabrina said coolly, her body stiff and unresponsive in his arms.

She could feel his muscles tauten against her like those of an animal sensing danger. "They usually do," he said warily, stepping back and turning her around to face him. "Except when there's a bad storm. Then the cottage becomes flooded and they have to vacate." His eyes were narrowed on her face.

"How unfortunate," Sabrina said caustically. "And they use *your* suite when they're driven here as orphans of the storm?"

"If I'm not on the island. Lance likes that bathtub," he answered absently. His hand tightened on her arms and his face was growing grimmer by the second. "What the hell difference does it make?"

It shouldn't make any difference. Why was she pushing like this? Why couldn't she just leave it alone? It was as if something was goading her to strike out at him.

"No difference," she said tartly. "I'd just feel more comfortable if you remembered who occupied your bed the last time you were here. It doesn't promise well for the future, does it?"

"I thought we'd settled all that," he said, giving her a little shake. "Why are you doing this, Sabrina?"

There was a tightness about his face and a smoldering anger in his eyes that she hadn't seen there for a long time. "It was a shock, I suppose," she said brittlely. "I wasn't expecting to run into this particular skeleton in your closet." She was speaking rapidly, almost feverishly. "Or should I say bureau? You must give me a tour and let me know what to avoid. I wouldn't want you to think I was invading your privacy."

"You can tear the damn house apart looking for traces of my lurid past for all I care," he said roughly, and the smolder had definitely burst into flame. "Damn it, I don't know who that nightgown belongs to if it's not Honey's! I don't remember having another woman here on the island, but what difference does it make if I did? I can't wipe out the past and I've no intention of apologizing for anything that happened before you came on the scene."

"I'm not asking you to apologize," she said, smiling brightly, her face stiff and frozen. "I've just decided I need a little more time to think about all this."

Oh Lord, why was she saying this? Ten minutes ago she'd wanted nothing more in the world than to be in Alex's arms. Why couldn't she forget the faceless woman who'd worn that little bit of nothing?

"Well, you're not going to get it," Alex said angrily.

"This is crazy, Sabrina. Since the moment we met you've been telling me what a cynical bastard I am, and how you can't involve yourself with me because I don't have the capacity to trust. Well, I've been beating my brains out trying to give you what you want from me. Good Lord, I haven't even *mentioned* that cowboy you're so committed to since that night at the ranch!" He shook her harder. "Do you have any conception of how difficult that's been for me? But I've met your damn test, and there's no way you're backing away from me now."

"I'm not backing a—"

"The hell you're not," he interrupted. "Do you think I couldn't feel you pulling away from me every time I mentioned anything resembling permanency in our relationship? I tried to ignore it, and told myself that as soon as you were sure of me all that hesitancy would go away. I've done everything I could think of to show you what you mean to me. What else do you want from me?"

"Is it too much to ask you to give me a little more time?" Sabrina asked desperately, trying to shake off his hold.

"You bet it's too much," he said tersely. "Because it's not jealousy, and it's surely not any reluctance to go to bed with me that's causing you to act this way. You're frightened, Sabrina."

"Why should I be frightened?" she asked, moistening her lips nervously. "I told you I was through being intimidated by you, Alex."

"You *are* scared," he said slowly, his eyes narrowing on her face. "Why the hell didn't I realize it before? It's *you* who doesn't trust what we've found together. I realized a long time ago it was strong enough to take anything life could throw at us, but you still have your doubts." He drew a deep breath. "I'm throwing the same challenge back at you, Sabrina. Trust me. And I'm raising the pot. Love me. For as God is my witness, I love *you*." His hands dropped from her shoulders and he stepped back. "Think about it." As he turned away from her, his face was harsher than she'd ever seen it. "I'm going down to the terrace, but I'll be damned if I'll wait long before I come after you." The door closed behind him with a firmness that was almost a slam.

Sabrina stared blankly at the door, as stunned and bewildered as if he'd slapped her. Could it be true? She dropped into the empress chair, gazing unseeingly before her. Alex's words had affected her deeply; it could well be he'd uncovered a truth she'd hidden even from herself. She sat until the golden rays of the late afternoon sun had faded to the melancholy lavender of twilight, her mind feverishly replaying her actions since she'd met him.

Good Lord, how cowardly could a person be. She'd always thought she'd have the courage and strength to face anything, but she hadn't even passed the first test after she'd realized her love for Alex. First she'd run away, and then after they'd made love and he was edging her too close to a commitment, she'd shifted the burden completely on his shoulders, skirting her own personal apprehensions. He was right. She'd been afraid to trust him, afraid to tell him about David and her responsibility that might last a lifetime. And today when she'd subconsciously realized it was really love Alex felt for her, she'd tried to push him away again with that idiotic fit of jealousy.

How could she have been so blind—even to let Alex subdue his pride and be the first one to say the words that put a label on this magical bond between them. Love. What a beautiful word, and how harsh he had sounded saying it. She was at fault there as well, but she could at least make this right.

She rose suddenly to her feet and started determinedly for the door. She was through running away. She'd given so generously to David of her faith and her love but she'd been positively miserly with those gifts with Alex. Well, it was time for a change and she knew just how she was going to signal that change to him.

Nine

Forty minutes later she'd finished showering and brushing her hair until it was a shimmering, fiery veil about her shoulders. Then she set about removing the evidence of those three freckles Alex had commented upon. The pixie would have to go, it was glamour she wanted tonight. After another ten minutes with mascara, eye shadow, and a touch of lip gloss, it was glamour she had.

Now for something to wear. The nightgown that Alex had chosen in Corpus Christi would be just right for her purpose. Its ivory satin sheen was not only complimentary to her figure and coloring, but though cut in the deceptively clinging style of the thirties it was really quite full. She'd need every bit of that fullness. She cast a last, critical glance at the mirror and nodded with satisfaction. She'd never looked more alluring in her life.

Then she was snatching the cassette tape Clancy had returned to her and hastening out of the bedroom and down the stairs. She stopped only long enough to grab Alex's portable cassette player from the library before hurrying toward the French doors that led to the terrace. She paused there for a moment and drew a deep breath, aware suddenly of butterflies in her stomach. Strange—she'd never been nervous before a performance in her entire career. But then no performance had ever been as important as this one.

She slowly opened the door and stood there silently for a moment. Alex was standing with his back to her at the balustrade, looking out at the wine dark sea, and the full moon lent an almost daylight clarity to the scene. The warm gentle breeze was lifting the dark silk of his hair, and it stirred a fugitive memory. Why hadn't she realized before that Lance Rubinoff's portrait of Alex had been painted on this terrace? But perhaps it hadn't been meant for her to know until now. At the moment it was easy to believe in a fate that would bring them full circle, from the portrait that was her first contact with Alex to this final confrontation.

She put the cassette player down on the glass breakfast table and though it made only a tiny scraping sound it was enough to cause Alex to whirl on her, with a wariness that filled her with remorse. There was a crackling tension she could feel across the space between them. What had he been thinking while he'd waited for her to come down?

Whatever it was, she couldn't read it in the shadowed tautness of his face as he gazed at her for a moment that seemed to last forever. Then he gave a long, deep sigh that was almost a shudder. "Where's Huckleberry Finn?" he asked huskily.

"I sent him on vacation." She smiled with loving tenderness. "You know how he likes to go adventuring. I told him I'd keep you company. I don't think you'll mind the substitution."

"Somehow I don't think I will either," he said thickly, his gaze flickering over her hungrily. "Why don't you come over here and let me find out?"

"Soon," she promised lightly. "But first I have something to give you. It's in the nature of a farewell performance." Her finger touched the button on the tape recorder and the terrace was suddenly alive with the throbbing syncopation of sensuous music. With a movement as graceful as the lifting of swallow's wings, her arms rose above her head.

It was a poignantly beautiful dance at the beginning, moving as a stately ballet. She improvised as she went along, wanting to give him something as exquisitely meaningful as the love she felt for him. Then, as the tempo accelerated, she exploded into a passionate, sensual litany of desire. She was vaguely aware of Alex's tense figure as she whirled and gyrated. Her shimmering hair whipped about her sinuous body like a flame.

For the man watching her, the dance seemed to go on for an eternity and each minute the desire for that flame of a woman was mounting to an almost unbearable pitch. Then when he thought that he could stand no more the music came to an end with a triumphant crash of cymbals, and Sabrina was kneeling before him in traditional obeisance.

Her breasts were heaving and her emerald eyes shining like stars as she looked up at him. "I have a present for you, Alex Ben Raschid," she said softly. "All my love. All my trust. Forever." Then, before he could answer, she was on her feet and running down the terrace steps to the path leading to the beach.

"Sabrina!"

Only a laugh answered him as she fled, all moonlight satin and flame, racing down the hill as if on wings. She didn't look back but she knew Alex was following and she laughed again. She was so filled with excitement and a heady euphoria, she felt as if at any moment she would leave the ground and fly away. Her bare feet skimmed over soft, cushioning sand still warm from the sun, until she reached the palm-shaded hillock where they'd stopped that afternoon.

It seemed a lifetime ago, she thought as she turned and waited for Alex. He was only a few yards behind and in an instant she was in his arms, his lips covering her face with hot, scorching kisses. His chest was heaving from the chase, but the little breath he had he gave to her, as their lips clung with a passion that was painfully intense.

"No," She broke away from him and hurriedly backed away. "Not that way."

"Sabrina." Alex drew a deep, shuddering breath, and his hands clenched at his sides. "My God, I can't take much more. *Any* way, damn it!"

He looked so taut and strained that for an instant she was tempted to fly back into his arms. But no, she wanted more for him than that.

"I want it to be right," she said gently, and slowly reached up to slide the satin straps of her gown from her shoulders. She let the bodice fall to her waist, feeling the warm breeze caress the swollen tautness of her breasts. Then with painstaking deliberation she slowly slid the gown over her hips, and let it fall in a shimmering ivory pool to the sand. "The performance isn't over yet, Alex."

She flowed toward him, her naked flesh shining in the moonlight like the satin gown she'd just discarded. She stopped before him and her hands reached out. He stood there, his body tense, scarcely breathing as she unbuttoned his shirt with steady hands. Strange they should be steady when she was quivering so inside.

"I don't suppose you'd let me help you," Alex rasped, as she pushed the shirt from his shoulders and down over his arms.

She shook her head, her hair caressing his bare

chest. "No." She brushed a kiss in the hollow of his shoulder. "I want to do everything for you." Her hands were at his belt and unfastening his pants, while her lips traced a multitude of light, teasing kisses across his chest and the springy dark pelt that narrowed to a fine line at his waist. Her lips traced that line while she impatiently pushed his khakis and briefs over his hips, falling to her knees to complete the task. Then he was tearing off his shoes and socks so that he was as naked as the woman kneeling before him.

"You know, of course, that you're driving me crazy," he said hoarsely. "Chinese water torture is mild compared to this." He jerked suddenly as her tongue seared an extremely sensitive area. "Sabrina!"

Then she was on her feet, her arms sliding over his shoulders to curl in the silky hair at his nape. "Well, you did once promise I could taste you all over," she whispered mischievously. "Aren't you a man of your word?"

"Later," he groaned, as his arms went around her, his hands cupping her buttocks and lifting her against his iron-hard arousal. "Much later. I can't exist another minute without being inside you, love."

As he lifted her higher her legs instinctively curled around his hips, and then with a frantic adjustment he plunged home, reaching his goal with a savage explosiveness that took her breath away.

"Alex!" Her arms tightened around his neck and her head fell to his shoulder. The sensation was unbelievable. For a moment she felt joined to a runaway comet, splitting the universe as it ran its fiery circuit. Then Alex was moving and the universe was being reborn with a power and velocity that made her gasp. She didn't remember when he sank to his knees in the sand. She was too dazzled by the physical and emotional responses he was wringing from her with each bold thrust and tactile manipulation of her body.

"Lord, little flame, I can't stand it," Alex gasped. "I've never known anything like this in my life. The whole world is exploding!"

Then the world did explode, but neither of them cared when there was a galaxy of pleasure to be gathered from each rapturous movement, each lingering kiss, every stroking caress whose denouement was as beautiful as the climax before it.

Then they lay sated and dreamily euphoric in each other's arms, joined in a union as blissfully peaceful as the other had been tempestuous.

"Alex?"

"Hmmm?"

"Did you like my performance?"

She could hear his deep chuckle beneath her ear as his hand gently stroked the hair at her temple. "Your solo was absolutely superb but it was our duet that really blew my mind. I can't wait for the encore."

"Alex?"

"Hmmm?"

"I hate to mention it, but this sand is tickling my back," Sabrina said, shifting her shoulders to find a more comfortable position.

"I can see right now what a shrew of a wife you're going to be." Alex sighed, a smile on his lips as he looked down at her. "What other woman would have the nerve to complain after I'd given her my very best."

"Was that your best, Alex?" Sabrina asked, her eyes twinkling. "I was hoping that practice would make perfect."

"And now you're insulting my expertise," he said in mock indignation. There was a sudden mischievous glint in his eyes. "Well let's just see if it was, shall we?" His hands moved down to cup her buttocks, and, holding her securely chained to his body, he suddenly rolled over so that she was on top of him.

"Alex, what are you doing?" Sabrina gasped, as he leisurely reached up to cup her breasts in his hands, his thumbs teasing her nipples into taut prominence.

"Enjoying myself," he answered promptly. "You were so involved with teasing *me* before that you didn't let me play with *you*." He lifted his head to capture one engorged nipple in his lips and nibbled at it with tongue and teeth. "Have I ever told you how much I love your breasts?"

"I believe you have mentioned it," she choked. Who would have thought, after that first wild, exhilarating culmination, that she could want him again so soon. She felt a sudden bold stirring within her and her eyes widened in amazement. "Alex?"

"Why are you so surprised?" He chuckled. "You should be aware of the effect you have on me by this time." He sat up suddenly and swiftly lifted her legs and wrapped them around his hips. "I think you're right, this sand is a little uncomfortable. Hang on tight. I don't want to lose you, love."

She clutched desperately at his shoulders and her legs clamped automatically around him as he got to his feet. "Alex, I don't understand what—" She broke off, unable to speak, while incredible pounding sensations surged through her as he ran with her down the short stretch of beach to the rolling surf.

Then, as Alex waded forcefully into the sea, she was deluged by a complexity of sensations that made her light-headed: The first shocking chill of the water against her warm flesh, the silky flow of currents around them, and the hot friction of their bodies as Alex started to *move.*

Later, she couldn't have said how long that wild, heated union lasted in those moonlit waters, but she was so weary when Alex carried her back to the beach that she could scarcely lift her head. She was vaguely aware of being set gently down on the sand, then he was putting her arms into the sleeves of his brown cotton shirt.

"Where are we going?" she asked drowsily, as he scooped her up in his arms and started rapidly across the sand.

"Back to the house," he answered, brushing her temple with a gentle kiss. "I don't want you to get a chill. Just relax and let me do everything for a change."

She wasn't about to argue, when it seemed too much trouble to wriggle even a finger. She snuggled closer to him, his heartbeat a reassuring metronome beneath her ear. "You don't have any clothes on," she observed. "Won't you be cold?"

"With you in my arms?" he asked mockingly. "No way, little flame."

"That's very complimentary, if not precisely accurate." She chuckled. "This time I'm *sure* I've had your best."

"Are you?" There was a glint of mischief in his eyes as he looked down at her. "You shouldn't ever be that positive of anything without in-depth research. Look what I had to contend with in that sea tonight. Currents, water temperature, not to mention keeping both of us from drowning." He cocked his head as if considering. "No, upon reflection, I'd say I operate much more effectively in a bathtub. Shall we try it when we get back to the house?"

"Later, perhaps," she answered lazily. "I don't think I could move a muscle at the moment."

"Would you like to make a small wager?" he asked, and then as her eyes widened in disbelief, he shook his head. "Sorry, love. I can't seem to get enough of you. You're right, we'll go to bed and I'll let you rest."

"You don't have to give in so easily," she pouted in mock disappointment. "I thought you'd at least put up a fight." Then her expression became grave. "I need to talk to you, Alex. There's something I have to tell you."

"Not tonight," he said softly, his arms tightening around her. "We have the next fifty years or so to talk. You said everything that was important on the terrace. Love. Trust. Forever. Nothing else really matters, does it?"

"No, I guess it doesn't," Sabrina said huskily, nestling still closer to his dear, hard warmth. "Nothing else is really important but that."

She didn't realize until later what sound pierced the veil of her exhausted slumber, but suddenly she was wide-awake and sitting bolt upright in the king-sized bed. Her heart raced as if she'd been running. "Alex, did you—"

Alex! The pillow still retained the impression of his head but the covers on his side of the bed looked as if they'd been hurriedly tossed aside. She felt a chill of panic run through her and drew a deep, steadying breath. He was probably in the bathroom. Nothing was wrong, she assured herself. But the bathroom door was still open the way he had flung it when he'd carried her to bed from that outrageously sybaritic tub, and the bathroom was dark. And somehow she didn't think he would have left her for any but the most urgent of reasons. Those last moments before they'd fallen asleep had been so poignantly tender. . . . Damn it, where was he?

She was out of bed and across the room with a speed that reflected the frightening answer that had just occurred to her. Four kidnap attempts, Clancy had said. Her hands searched frantically through the closet until she found Alex's white terrycloth robe. Oh, God, and three assassination attempts! Why hadn't she insisted on the security men being quartered on the island? She shrugged herself into the robe and was tying the belt as she reached the door. She was probably crazy—and Alex would be downstairs safe and sound. Oh, God, let that be true!

Her bare feet skimmed down the hall and at the head of the stairs she gave a sigh of relief. The foyer was brightly lit, and so was the living room opening off it. Of course Alex was all right, how idiotic to imagine he could be snatched away in the middle of the night without her even being aware of it.

"Alex, why didn't you wake me?" she called, as she reached the bottom of the stairs. "Do you know how frigh—"

She broke off as Clancy Donahue, dressed in worn jeans and a disreputable navy sweatshirt, strode out of the living room into the foyer. His expression was set and grim. Sabrina's breath stopped in her breast. "Clancy, what are you doing here? Where's Alex?"

"At the moment I'm fixing myself a drink," he said gruffly. "Come on, I think I'd better fix you one, too." Then, at her horrified gasp, he said quickly. "Alex is fine. I didn't mean to frighten you."

"Well, you did," Sabrina said indignantly. "First you pump me full of warnings and forebodings, then Alex disappears, and you tell me I'm going to need a drink. How do you expect me to react?"

"I said I was sorry," Clancy said defensively, taking her elbow and propelling her into the living room. "I've never claimed diplomacy is my strong point. I spoke without thinking, I guess I'm a little upset."

"Upset?" Sabrina asked in exasperation. "Clancy, where *is* Alex?"

"On his way to Sedikhan," Clancy answered tersely.

Sabrina could feel the blood drain from her face. "Sedikhan?" she asked haltingly.

Clancy hurriedly pushed her down on a yellow, cushioned bar stool. "I thought you might need that drink," he said, picking up the snifter of brandy he'd poured for himself and thrusting it at her. "Now don't go jumping to conclusions. He had to go, damn it."

"In the middle of the night?" Sabrina asked blankly. "Without any warning?" She set the brandy down on the bar without tasting it. "Without telling me?"

"That was supposed to be my job," Clancy replied gloomily. "And I'm not doing it very well, am I?" He scowled. "I don't know why he couldn't have done it himself. He said you were tired and he didn't want to wake you. Yet the blasted copter barely gets off the ground and you're down here asking me quesions."

The helicopter. It must have been the helicopter taking off that had awakened her, she thought dazedly. "Why did he have to return to Sedikhan?"

"His grandfather," Clancy answered. "The doctors think Karim may have suffered a heart attack. They don't know how serious his condition is yet, but apparently it's grave enough for them to send for Alex." He picked up the brandy snifter she'd refused and took a sip. "I received a radiogram aboard the yacht a couple of hours ago and came by launch to give Alex the word."

"I see," she said slowly. "I'm sorry to hear that. Alex is very fond of his grandfather, isn't he?"

Donahue nodded. "They're as close as two exceptionally strong personalities can be," he replied. "They care for each other, but for the most part find it more comfortable to be half a world apart." His lips curved wryly. "I wouldn't be too concerned if I were you. Karim's a tough old bird. He'll probably live to be a hundred."

A sudden thought occurred to her. "Why didn't you go with him?" she said, frowning accusingly at him. "You said Alex's enemies would find a situation like this tailor-made, yet you let him go off alone."

"He's not alone," Clancy said sulkily. "He'll have half the security force of Sedikhan at his disposal once he steps off the plane."

"I still think you should have—"

"So do I, damn it!" he interrupted. He crashed the snifter down on the bar. "Do you think I like the idea of letting him go off without me? He's never before turned down my help in a tight spot." He glowered at her. "Until now. I have orders to stay here and look after you."

Sabrina's mouth fell open. "Me?" she said, her eyes widening. "Why should you take care of me? Alex is the one in danger."

"That's what I tried to tell him," Clancy growled. "He wouldn't listen to me. He said he wouldn't take the chance of leaving you alone and unprotected on the island. So I'm stuck here playing bodyguard to you until Alex comes back."

"And when will that be?" she asked.

He shrugged. "Who knows? It depends on how ill Karim turns out to be. A week or two perhaps."

She shook her head. "I can't stay here that long. I promised I'd be back at the Bradfords' on Monday."

"Call them and tell them you've been delayed," he said promptly. "Alex gave me orders you weren't to leave the island until he could come back to you."

"Orders?" Sabrina bristled, her eyes narrowing. "I don't like orders, as Alex is very well aware. You can't keep me on the island if I don't want to be here, Clancy."

"Look, Alex didn't have the time to observe all the courtesies, Sabrina," Clancy said impatiently. "His grandfather may be dying, remember?"

Sabrina felt a surge of remorse. He was right. It wasn't fair of her to be annoyed with Alex when he'd undoubtedly been worried and distracted. And his arrogance was too ingrained for him to change overnight. There would probably be many compromises for them both to make in the future. But it didn't change the fact that she'd made a promise to David.

"I can understand why he was upset," she said gently. "But I've got to keep my promise, Clancy." She stood up and tightened her robe. "I'm going upstairs to get dressed now. Will you take me back to Houston?"

"Alex will have my head if I do," Clancy said gloomily. His face was troubled as he continued awkwardly, "Maybe it's none of my business, but I'm going to have my say anyway. Don't go back to that cowboy just because you're upset with Alex for leaving you like this. I think that was what Alex was worried about when he ordered me to keep you here. He doesn't want to lose you."

"He isn't going to lose me," she said softly. "And when he's had time to think about it he's going to know that."

"Not if you go back to the Bradford ranch," Clancy said flatly. "He's jealous as hell of that guy you've been living with." He frowned. "Don't do it, kid. Alex really cares for you. I think he would have taken you with him to Sedikhan if it hadn't been safer for you here." Clancy glanced away. "I had to go up to your bedroom to wake Alex, you know." His gaze shifted back to her and though there was a flush on his cheeks, his eyes were suspiciously bright. "You needn't blush like that," he said gruffly. "What I saw in that bed was nothing to be embarrassed about. The two of you are beautiful together, and Alex's face, when he was looking down at you, was beautiful, too." He scowled. "Don't you dare tell him I said that, he'll think I'm going soft. But it *was* beautiful, damn it, as if he were all lit up inside."

"I won't tell him," Sabrina promised huskily. "But I can't stay here either, Clancy." She smiled reassuringly. "Don't worry, it's going to be all right. There aren't going to be any more misunderstandings from now on. We've gotten past that point."

He cast her a distinctly skeptical glance. "Maybe *you* have, but I'm not at all sure about Alex." He sighed resignedly. "I'm not going to talk you out of it, am I?"

She shook her head. "No, I have to leave," she said quietly. Then her emerald eyes glinted teasingly. "Besides, with me safely tucked away at the ranch, you can join Alex in Sedikhan. You know that's what you want to do anyway."

"That's right, I could," Clancy said, brightening. He made a face. "Not that Alex won't make my life hell on earth when he finds out I've let you go back to Bradford. What the hell am I going to say to him?"

"You're going to give him a message from me,"

she said serenely. "Tell him I'll be waiting for him to come to me."

"That's all?" Clancy asked, surprised.

She was already striding swiftly toward the door. She paused in the doorway and a gentle smile lit her face. "Not quite," she said softly. "Three more words. Love. Trust. Forever."

Then she turned and left the room.

Ten

"Bree, why wouldn't you speak to that man on the telephone this morning?" David asked, a troubled frown creasing his forehead. "Dad says he was calling all the way from London."

"Alex?" Sabrina looked up from her weeding to smile at him. "I just thought it best. Did you think I was being rude, love?"

David shook his head. "I knew you must have a good reason," he said slowly. He carefully plucked a weed that was encroaching on a young slip. "I'd just never heard you refuse to speak to anyone before, and then you told Dad to tell him you'd expect to see him this evening. It confused me. Don't you like him, Bree?"

"Yes, I like him very much," Sabrina said softly. "And I think you will, too." She moved a few inches to pull at another weed. "I just thought it would be simpler if he came to the ranch to talk to me."

"I thought you must like him a lot to go away on a trip with him," David said gravely, wiping his hands absently on the knees of his faded Levi's as he sat back on his heels. "And then when you came back you told me we were going to wait a few weeks before leaving the ranch." David's expression was puzzled. "Is this what we've been waiting for, Bree?"

"Yes, this is what we've been waiting for, David," she said quietly. "Have you minded staying here these extra weeks?"

"No, I didn't mind. It gave me a chance to put in this flower garden for Mother. Now all she'll have to do is nurture and guard it after I leave."

"I'm sure the garden will make her very happy," Sabrina said gently. It had been impossible not to notice the aura of strain about Sue in the last two weeks, but David had seemed oddly serene and happy. Perhaps working with his beloved plants had helped assuage the pain and bewilderment of his mother's rejection. "You never told me what you planted in her garden, love." Sabrina motioned with her trowel to the bushes bordering the house. "Besides the roses, of course."

"I tried to plan it," he said eagerly. "This row is red chrysanthemums, I've planted pinks over there, and white myrtle by the screen door."

"It sounds lovely," Sabrina said. "And what's underneath the kitchen window? I noticed you spent hours landscaping that particular spot."

His gaze followed hers to the brick-bordered alcove and he smiled gently. "I've planted blue forget-me-nots and rosemary there, Bree."

The smile faded from Sabrina's face. Forget-me-nots. And everyone knew rosemary meant remembrance. David certainly did. She remembered the night he'd excitedly brought up that old horticulture magazine of Gino's to show her the chart with all the flower meanings on it.

"Why rosemary, David?" she asked quietly.

"So she'll remember me," he said simply. "I thought about it a long time, Bree. I know we probably won't be coming back here again. Isn't that right?"

What could she say to him? "Probably not, David."

"I didn't think so," he said, and for a moment there was a poignant wistfulness in his eyes. "That's why I planted the garden." He bit his lip. "Do you remember what I said about me not really being there for her, Bree?"

"Yes, I remember, love."

"Well, I figured this was one way I could be there." His forehead knotted in concentration. "And it won't hurt her to look at my flowers and think of me, will it?"

"No, I think it will make her very happy," Sabrina said huskily, her eyes brimming with tears. "What do all the other flowers mean?"

"Love," he said simply. "They all mean love. That's all I really wanted to say."

A garden of love and remembrance. Could there ever be a more beautiful gift? David had overcome his own pain and found a way to ease his mother's unhappiness. The quiet serenity she'd seen in him these past two weeks had been hard won.

She drew a deep, steadying breath and lowered her eyes. She wouldn't weaken him with her tears. "Will you show Alex your garden when he gets here this evening?" she asked lightly.

"If you want me to," he said. "Does he like flowers, Bree?"

"I don't imagine he knows much about them," she admitted cheerfully. "But I'm sure he would enjoy hearing about Miranda and your plants in Houston as well."

"Okay," he said eagerly, his face brightening. "Maybe I'll take him down to the stable to see my horse. Does he ride?"

"I don't even know," she said with a grin. "Why don't you ask him?"

"I will." His face once more darkened in a worried frown. "Are you sure he'll like me? I want him to."

"He'll like you," she assured him gently. Then, as he continued to frown, she added gravely, "Do you remember what you told me a few weeks ago, about how wonderful it would be if all we had to do was reach out and touch to make one another bloom?"

He nodded slowly.

"Well, Alex is one of those who will bloom if you touch him, David. On the outside he's all closed up and guarded, but when he unfolds his petals, he's beautiful." She smiled, her expression serene. "Now if you'll excuse me, I'll leave you to do the rest of this weeding on your own. I'd like to be on my way before it gets dark."

"You're not going to be here?" David asked, surprised.

She shook her head. "I'm going to the Circle C," she said quietly. "I want you to get to know each other and I think it will be easier if you're alone. Will you tell Alex I'll be waiting there for him?"

David nodded. "He won't be angry, will he?"

"Perhaps a little," she said calmly. "But he won't be when he understands."

"If you say so," he said absently. "Look, Bree." His finger gently touched one green sprig. "We bury them in the earth and yet they fight their way to the sun. It's a miracle. Who could believe something so beautiful could come out of the darkness."

"I believe it," she said, her gaze on the gentle wonder radiating from his face. She turned leaving David to continue to nurture his garden of love.

When Sabrina parked the Volkswagen in front of the ranch house it was already sunset. There wasn't much left to do, thank heaven. She'd come over earlier in the week and swept and scrubbed the room until it sparkled. Now she went directly

from the dim hallway into the living room, and lit
the logs she'd carefully laid in the fireplace. Soon
there was a crackling blaze.

Then she set about lighting the candles. It took
her a long time, for she'd garnered every empty
wine and soda bottle she could find at the Bradfords', wrapped them in glittering silver foil, and
mounted a white candle in each one. There wasn't
much she could do to make this large, empty
room look festive, but she wanted Alex to know as
soon as he came in that she regarded his home-
coming as a celebration. When she finished ar-
ranging the candles, she gave a contented sigh.
Their dancing shadows played on the walls, and
they lit the darkness like a birthday cake. Yes,
Alex would know she was celebrating.

She moved to the fireplace and dropped down
on the cushions she'd carefully covered with a
crisp, cotton sheet. She kicked off her sandals
and tucked her blouse into the waist of her jeans.
She'd deliberately dressed as casually as possible
but hadn't been able to resist wearing this simple,
white poet's blouse with its extravagantly full
sleeves that buttoned at the wrist. It gave her the
romantic air of a corsair and exactly matched her
mood tonight. Crossing her legs tailor fashion,
she settled herself patiently to wait.

The candles were almost half burned and she'd
had to twice restoke the fire before she heard the
car pull up outside. Then there was the sound of
swift, firm footsteps on the porch, the front door
was thrown violently open, and she felt her breath
stop and her heart turn over. God, she had missed
him! It seemed more like a year than two weeks
since that night on the island.

Then he was there, lighting the room with a
vitality brighter than her candles. His close-fitting
black jeans hugged the strong line of his thighs

and the sleeves of his black sports shirt were rolled carelessly to the elbow. His dark silky hair was rumpled and there was a grim frown on his face.

He halted in surprise, his gaze wandering about the room. When he finally zeroed in on Sabrina, an amused smile replaced his frown. "You never cease to amaze me, Sabrina," he said, shaking his head ruefully. "I come tearing in here fully prepared to shake the living daylights out of you and you meet me with this! How the hell am I supposed to stay angry with you?"

"You're not," she said softly, her eyes running lovingly over his face. He looked tired. His skin was stretched taut, throwing his cheekbones into bold prominence, and around his mouth were deep lines of tension. "Why were you angry with me?" she asked.

"Why do you think?" He scowled. "You disobeyed my orders and left the island. You refused to take any of my telephone calls, and let me go through hell wondering why you'd returned to Bradford. You knew I couldn't leave Sedikhan until my grandfather was well enough to assume control again. Yet you let me simmer for two agonizing weeks."

"I'm glad your grandfather is better," she said quietly. "I read in the newspaper that he's almost completely recovered now. There were some rumors he might be thinking of abdicating in your favor."

His lips twisted derisively. "Not very likely. As long as he can stand on his own two feet, he's not about to give up even a smidgeon of the power he wields." Alex shrugged. "Which suits me just fine. There's more than enough for the two of us." He paused. "I told him about you."

"You did?" Her eyes widened in surprise.

He nodded. "Hell, I couldn't hide the fact that I

was chomping at the bit to get back to you." He smiled wryly. "He pumped Clancy of all he knew about you and then tackled me. He doesn't approve of the way I've handled our entire affair, incidentally."

"How unfortunate," she said, her lips curving in amusement at the idea of Alex forced to sit tamely while his grandfather gave him advice to the lovelorn.

"He thinks I should have had you kidnapped and then kept you in a lovenest somewhere until I'd gotten you pregnant." Alex spoke solemnly, but with a glint of mischief in the depths of his night dark eyes. "I have to admit that the idea appealed to me." His expression darkened. "Particularly when you let me go through that entire time without a word."

"I sent you word," she reminded him gently. "In fact, I sent you three of them. Remember?"

"I remember," he growled. "It was the only thing I had to hang on to for two blasted weeks. You expected a lot from me, Sabrina. I'm still amateur status at this trust business. I very nearly sent one of my men to bring you to me."

"But you didn't," she said quietly. "That's pretty impressive going for an amateur."

He came to her now. "I'm glad you appreciate my progress," he said, grimacing ruefully. "But you knew how jealous I was of Bradford."

"Yes, I knew that," she said quietly, as he sat on the cushion facing her. "But it was a difficult situation to explain." She unconsciously tensed. "You've talked to David?"

"Yes," he said absently. His hand reached out to touch the collar of her poet's blouse. "I like this. When I walked in the door, I didn't know if I'd find my Huckleberry Finn or a flame in white satin. Instead I find a court page from another century.

I never know what to expect from you." He moved his hand to stroke her cheek with mesmerizing gentleness.

"I talked to Bradford and his wife and I'm sure they told me everything you wanted them to," Alex went on quietly. "And then I had a long talk with your David. We discussed his garden and Gino and Angelina. He told me about a daffodil named Miranda and his best friend, Bree, who was like a beautiful poinsettia."

"He told you that?"

Alex nodded, his lips tightening grimly. "He was a hell of a lot more confiding than his precious Bree. Why couldn't you have just told me about him? Did you think I was such an insensitive bastard that I wouldn't see how special he is?"

"I was frightened," she said simply. "I'd never loved anyone the way I loved you, and I suppose I was subconsciously afraid you'd reject David." Her gaze was direct. "You do realize that it's a package deal, Alex? There's no way I can desert David now."

"I'd be a fool not to realize that after meeting the boy," he said gruffly. He stroked the silky hair at her temple. "You couldn't desert anyone you cared about."

"And you know it may be for the rest of our lives?"

"I realize that." His hand dropped to her shoulder and he met her eyes with a gravity and tenderness that caused her throat to tighten achingly. "I love you. You're the other half of me, remember? I could no sooner reject someone who was important to you than I could cut off my right arm. I want to shoulder all your burdens if you'll let me, love." He frowned, his eyes narrowed thoughtfully. "The first thing we'll do is round up the best damn doctors in the world and work at getting him well."

She should have expected that from Alex, Sabrina thought tenderly. He'd never be content until he'd exhausted every possibility. "He may never be any better," she said quietly. "The doctors just don't know, Alex."

"Well, they will before I'm finished," he said arrogantly. "And one of them had better find a way to help him." Then, as she chuckled irrepressibly, he grinned a bit sheepishly. "Sorry. I just can't bear the thought of the waste of a human being like David."

"And if the doctors can't help?" she asked.

His face softened and his dark eyes glowed with the tenderness that had made Clancy call him beautiful. "Then I'll set about creating him the most exquisite garden on the face of the earth," he said gently. "And we'll let him plant it with love. Then we'll nurture it and protect it all the days of our lives. Enough?"

"Enough," she said huskily, blinking rapidly. "I'm sorry. I think I'm going to cry."

"No, you're not," he said firmly, taking her in his arms and cradling her with poignant gentleness. "I won't have it."

She laughed throatily, tightening her arms about him. "I think you've stayed a little too long in Sedikhan," she said teasingly. "You're obviously going to be unbearably autocratic until I get you straightened out again." He felt so good. His lean sinewy warmth, the scent of soap and that woodsy cologne, the hard vital *feel* of him.

His lips brushed the pulse point just under her chin. "God, it seems like a century," he said thickly. "I'd lie in bed and think about that last night we had together and I thought I'd go up in flames. I was sure I'd have you in bed five minutes after I walked through this door."

"Then you're considerably behind schedule," she said softly, pressing her lips to the hollow of his cheek. "Please feel free to call on me any time to help you put it right."

"Don't worry, I have every intention of doing just that," he said, running his hands on her back in an exquisitely gentle caress that was both soothing and arousing. "But I've discovered something absolutely astounding."

"You have?"

He nodded and pushed her away to gaze down at her tenderly. "As much as I'm aching to love you and have you respond in that wild, sweet way, I want to wait a little longer." His lips lowered to hers. "I want to sit before the fire with you and hold you in my arms. I want to stroke that shining red hair and hear you laugh. Then I want to talk about commitment and love and growing old together. Would that be all right with you, little flame?"

She couldn't speak over the lump in her throat but her emerald eyes were glowing with a radiance that was answer enough. He kissed her once again and then tucked her head into the hollow of his shoulder, his strong arm encircling her with loving protectiveness.

They were silent and content for several long, peaceful moments, and then, slowly, they began to speak, while a hundred candles blazed in joyous celebration around them.

THE EDITOR'S CORNER

Ti amo. Ich liebe dich. Je t'aime. I love you. Those words along with all the other magical words in our LOVESWEPT romances are read by women around the world. We thought you'd be interested to learn that our books are translated into lots of languages for publication in many, many countries. So you share our delicious stories with women everywhere: Australia, Germany, France, New Zealand, Sweden, Norway, the Philippines . . . I could go on and on. And fan mail reaches us with the most exotic postmarks—Selangor, Malaysia, for example. Those postmarks certainly conjure romantic images for us on the LOVESWEPT staff. It is deeply touching to know that the tenderness, humor, warmth, sensuality—all the elements of loving in our LOVESWEPT romances—are enjoyed equally by the reader in Kansas City and in Kuala Lumpur. Close your eyes. Can you imagine the globe circled by women touching hands, sharing the common belief that stories about loving relationships are the best entertainment of all? It's a beautiful image, isn't it?

Now from the universal to the particular—namely, the treats in store for you next month.

Heading off the April LOVESWEPT list is Joan Domning's fourth romance, **KIRSTEN'S INHERITANCE**, LOVESWEPT #29. This absolutely heartwarming story is set in the tiny town of Avlum, Minnesota, and features the colorful and sexy hero, Dr. Cory Antonelli. The darling doctor rocks the town Kirsten has grown up in. (His jogging clothes appear to be underwear to the small town folks amazed by his activities in their midst.) And he is so darkly handsome in a town of fair people of Scandinavian heritage that not a single thing he does can escape notice. Author Joan knows of what she speaks! She was born and raised in a community

(continued)

quite similar to the imaginary one in which she sets this charming book. There are creative twists galore in this love story that I feel sure you're going to add to your collection of "keepers."

OOO-h, that Iris Johansen! Better read **RETURN TO SANTA FLORES,** LOVESWEPT #40, with great care! It's always a challenge to try to figure out which of Iris's secondary characters has his or her own love story next, isn't it? One hint: maybe the way to a woman's heart is *not* via the palate, but another sense. Now, though, let's focus on the marvelous romance between Steve and Jenny in **RETURN TO SANTA FLORES.** First, you'll notice that the opening chapter takes place eight years before chapter two. It's almost a prologue to the story and a delightful innovation in the writing craft for this particular romance. Steve considers himself years too old and jaded for Jenny . . . but she won't take "no" for an answer. Her scrapes and Steve's last minute rescues become legendary around the hotel he owns, but through everything the real question still remains: can Steve resist Jenny's love? There is a comic scene in a motel bedroom in this, Iris's eighth romance, that is priceless!

What a pleasure to be able to introduce yet another talented newcomer as a LOVESWEPT author. **THE SOPHISTICATED MOUNTAIN GAL,** LOVESWEPT #41, is Joan Bramsch's first novel. And it's a "WOW" of a love story. Crissy Brant is one of the most vivacious and wide-ranging heroines we've published. She is an Ozark Mountain gal, but she's also a sophisticated and well-trained actress with a unique ability to create characters in many different voices. James Prince, a disillusioned ad man recently transplanted to Bransom, Missouri, has started a new life as a toy manufacturer. He falls in love first with Crissy in her role of Tulip Bloom, the Silver Dollar City storyteller . . . and soon he's in love with all the other Crissy Brants, too. But outsiders don't win trust easily and James has several strikes against him—so the path to true love for these two delightful characters is as hard to negotiate as a steep and stone-strewn mountain road. By the way, there is a twenty-plus page "temptation" scene in this book that I guarantee will knock your socks off! My, oh my! Welcome to LOVESWEPT, Joan Bramsch!

Sara Orwig's first LOVESWEPT, **AUTUMN FLAMES**, received wonderful fan mail! Now Sara's topped even that romance with **HEAT WAVE**, LOVESWEPT #42. Marilee O'Neil literally drops into Cole Chandler's lap. Imagine Cole's surprise when, while sunbathing nude, a hot air balloon piloted by Marilee plunks down in the middle of his swimming pool. She claims to lead a dull and ordinary life—and perhaps that was the case *before* she met Cole. But life is anything but ordinary around this extraordinary hero. From painting his house on his wheat farm, to tutoring his nephew, to single-handedly capturing two rustlers on his property, Marilee's existence simmers in Cole's company. It's the hottest summer Kansas has known in recorded history . . . but the weather is cool in comparison to the sizzling love affair between two touching human beings. Sara Orwig just gets better and better all the time!

It's a pleasure to work with all these fine LOVESWEPT authors and a pleasure to hear from you that you are enjoying the series so much!

Until next month, we send warmest good wishes,
Sincerely,

Carolyn Nichols

Carolyn Nichols
Editor
LOVESWEPT
Bantam Books, Inc.
666 Fifth Avenue
New York, NY 10103

LOVESWEPT

Love Stories you'll never forget by authors you'll always remember

☐	21603	**Heaven's Price** #1 Sandra Brown	$1.95
☐	21604	**Surrender** #2 Helen Mittermeyer	$1.95
☐	21600	**The Joining Stone** #3 Noelle Berry McCue	$1.95
☐	21601	**Silver Miracles** #4 Fayrene Preston	$1.95
☐	21605	**Matching Wits** #5 Carla Neggers	$1.95
☐	21606	**A Love for All Time** #6 Dorothy Garlock	$1.95
☐	21607	**A Tryst With Mr. Lincoln?** #7 Billie Green	$1.95
☐	21602	**Temptation's Sting** #8 Helen Conrad	$1.95
☐	21608	**December 32nd . . . And Always** #9 Marie Michael	$1.95
☐	21609	**Hard Drivin' Man** #10 Nancy Carlson	$1.95
☐	21610	**Beloved Intruder** #11 Noelle Berry McCue	$1.95
☐	21611	**Hunter's Payne** #12 Joan J. Domning	$1.95
☐	21618	**Tiger Lady** #13 Joan Domning	$1.95
☐	21613	**Stormy Vows** #14 Iris Johansen	$1.95
☐	21614	**Brief Delight** #15 Helen Mittermeyer	$1.95
☐	21616	**A Very Reluctant Knight** #16 Billie Green	$1.95
☐	21617	**Tempest at Sea** #17 Iris Johansen	$1.95
☐	21619	**Autumn Flames** #18 Sara Orwig	$1.95
☐	21620	**Pfarr Lake Affair** #19 Joan Domning	$1.95
☐	21621	**Heart on a String** #20 Carla Neggars	$1.95
☐	21622	**The Seduction of Jason** #21 Fayrene Preston	$1.95
☐	21623	**Breakfast In Bed** #22 Sandra Brown	$1.95
☐	21624	**Taking Savannah** #23 Becky Combs	$1.95
☐	21625	**The Reluctant Lark** #24 Iris Johansen	$1.95

Prices and availability subject to change without notice.

Buy them at your local bookstore or use this handy coupon for ordering:

Bantam Books, Inc., Dept. SW, 414 East Golf Road, Des Plaines, Ill. 60016

Please send me the books I have checked above. I am enclosing $_____ (please add $1.25 to cover postage and handling). Send check or money order—no cash or C.O.D.'s please.

Mr/Ms_____

Address _____

City/State_____ Zip_____

SW—3/84

Please allow four to six weeks for delivery. This offer expires 9/84.

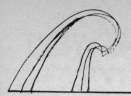

LOVESWEPT

Love Stories you'll never forget by authors you'll always remember

☐	21630	**LIGHTNING THAT LINGERS #25** Sharon & Tom Curtis	**$1.95**
☐	21631	**ONCE IN A BLUE MOON #26** Millie J. Green	**$1.95**
☐	21632	**THE BRONZED HAWK #27** Iris Johansen	**$1.95**
☐	21637	**LOVE, CATCH A WILD BIRD #28** Anne Reisser	**$1.95**
☐	21626	**THE LADY AND THE UNICORN #29** Iris Johansen	**$1.95**
☐	21628	**WINNER TAKE ALL #30** Nancy Holder	**$1.95**
☐	21635	**THE GOLDEN VALKYRIE #31** Iris Johansen	**$1.95**
☐	21638	**C.J.'s FATE #32** Kay Hooper	**$1.95**
☐	21639	**THE PLANTING SEASON #33** Dorothy Garlock	**$1.95**
☐	21629	**FOR LOVE OF SAMI #34** Fayrene Preston	**$1.95**
☐	21627	**THE TRUSTWORTHY REDHEAD #35** Iris Johansen	**$1.95**
☐	21636	**A TOUCH OF MAGIC #36** Carla Neggers	**$1.95**
☐	21641	**IRRESISTIBLE FORCES #37** Marie Michael	**$1.95**
☐	21642	**TEMPORARY ANGEL #38** Billie Green	**$1.95**
☐	21646	**KIRSTEN'S INHERITANCE #39** Joan Domning	**$1.95**
☐	21645	**RETURN TO SANTA FLORES #40** Iris Johansen	**$1.95**
☐	21656	**THE SOPHISTICATED MOUNTAIN GAL #41** Joan Bramsch	**$1.95**
☐	21655	**HEAT WAVE #42** Sara Orwig	**$1.95**

Prices and availability subject to change without notice.

Buy them at your local bookstore or use this handy coupon for ordering:

Bantam Books, Inc., Dept. SW, 414 East Golf Road, Des Plaines, Ill. 60016

Please send me the books I have checked above. I am enclosing $_____
(please add $1.25 to cover postage and handling). Send check or money order
—no cash or C.O.D.'s please.

Mr/Mrs/Miss _____

Address_____

City_____ State/Zip_____

SW2—4/84

Please allow four to six weeks for delivery. This offer expires 10/84.

SPECIAL
MONEY SAVING
OFFER

Now you can have an up-to-date listing of Bantam's hundreds of titles plus take advantage of our unique and exciting bonus book offer. A special offer which gives you the opportunity to purchase a Bantam book for only 50¢. Here's how!

By ordering any five books at the regular price per order, you can also choose any other single book listed (up to a $4.95 value) for just 50¢. Some restrictions do apply, but for further details why not send for Bantam's listing of titles today!

Just send us your name and address plus 50¢ to defray the postage and handling costs.